Julian Hawthorne

Section 558

The fatal letter. From the diary of Inspector Byrnes

Julian Hawthorne

Section 558
The fatal letter. From the diary of Inspector Byrnes

ISBN/EAN: 9783743463592

Manufactured in Europe, USA, Canada, Australia, Japa

Cover: Foto ©Andreas Hilbeck / pixelio.de

Manufactured and distributed by brebook publishing software (www.brebook.com)

Julian Hawthorne

Section 558

SECTION 558

OR

THE FATAL LETTER

FROM THE DIARY OF
INSPECTOR BYRNES

BY

JULIAN HAWTHORNE

AUTHOR OF "A TRAGIC MYSTERY," "THE GREAT BANK
ROBBERY," "AN AMERICAN PENMAN," ETC.

———

CASSELL & COMPANY, LIMITED,
104 & 106 FOURTH AVENUE, NEW YORK.

CONTENTS.

548

CONTENTS.

SECTION 558;

OR,

THE FATAL LETTER.

CHAPTER. I.

A WINTER FIRESIDE.

THERE had been a heavy fall of snow in New York city.

Snow wraps the earth in a veil of chilly purity; a purity not of youth and life, but of coldness and death. The heats of summer are forgotten; the royal hues of autumn have turned brown and withered; the tender verdure of spring seems distant and problematical; the blank winding-sheet of frozen white prevails over all things. We know that the ground underneath is hard, impenetrable and barren. The icy air comes keenly to the nostrils, and makes the flesh shrink and shiver. We turn our thoughts inward, and cease to court nature. She has left us, and we try to alleviate our loneliness by

huddling together round our fireside. Winter
is a selfish season, and it is well for our hearts
that Christmas comes in the midst of it,—a
new life of the soul in the midst of a physical
death. It is easy to be generous when the sun is
warm ; but during these bleak and bitter months
the unregenerate mind instinctively thinks first of
itself, and abandons the hindmost to the devil.

In winter the city homes of our rich people are
luxurious and splendid with all that wealth can
bestow ; and life glows with a sort of fierceness, as
if in defiance of the relentless chill out of doors.
The people who are not rich feel the pinch of poverty more cruelly than ever, and hesitate whether
to expend their beggarly coppers in food or in
fuel. As for the third estate—the criminals—
their brains and fingers are stimulated to especial
activity. Winter is the best time for stealing ;
property is then heaped together in greater masses
than at other seasons, and its owners sleep more
soundly. Besides, a thief can manage to pull
through the summer somehow, but in winter he
must live in the city and to do that money is indis-
pensable.

But the police are as active as the criminals, and
the battle between the two is fought uninterrupt-
edly from November till March. The courts are
kept busy, and the gaols are well stocked ; crime is
scotched, but not killed. That old serpent dies
hard, and is always thrusting up its ugly head in a
new place. Will it ever be conquered, and its

seed trodden out? Civilization only polishes and sharpens it. Religion seems to live side by side with it without embarrassment on either part: law inflicts penalties on it, but also defines its limitations so acutely that the criminal, now become learned in the law, uses it as an effective weapon for his own preservation. So the great tragi-comedy rolls along, and the planet, on its endless journey through unknown space, carries with it from year to year and from century to century an almost unvarying proportion of good and evil. We may lament that this evil is mixed with the good; but we must rejoice that there are always some traces of good in the evil.

The snow, which lay white and smooth outside the city, in the deserted fields and country roads, was speedily befouled in the great metropolis, until it wrought a filthiness even surpassing that of the rainy seasons. From brown it deepened to black, with something of the hideousness of a polluted corpse. It muddied the feet of the pedestrians as well as chilled them. In the lower part of the city, where the traffic is thickest, the nastiness was without mitigation. On Fifth Avenue the condition of things was not so bad. The sidewalks had been cleaned and the snow piled up in the roadway, affording fair sleighing for the graceful cutters that speeded up and down the stately thoroughfare. The people on the sidewalks were well and warmly clad, and altogether the spectacle had a certain brightness and cheerful vivacity. As night came on and the street lamps were lighted, the sleighs, with their jingling bells, disappeared, and only a few belated citizens hurried along the pavements.

Our present business demands that we accompany one of the latter.

When we first see him, he has just passed the Brunswick Hotel, and, keeping on the east side of the avenue, is walking northwards. His gait is swift and vigorous, betokening a powerful and healthy physical organization, and a concentrated and capable mind. He is evidently bound on some affair of importance ; indeed, when we contemplate the expression of his strong, ruddy, well-molded face, we are inclined to hazard the opinion that only affairs of importance ever engage his attention. He is a man whose life is full, earnest and active. He has no time to throw away ; and yet his time is so ordered that he is never unduly hurried or perplexed. Every year he does a year's work, and is fresh enough at the end of it to start on a new twelvemonth with undiminished energy.

He leaves behind him as he goes the fragrance of an excellent cigar. A thick overcoat is buttoned across his broad chest, a round-crowned hat is on his head, and his hands are encased in warm gloves. His eyes, without being restless, are at once penetrating and comprehensive in their glance, and take in quietly and easily every thing that lies within their range. He is a man whose wits are always with him. He has the air of good society, and yet there is something about him that distinguishes him from the ordinary " society man.": We feel that he must have raised himself in some way above the common level, that his name, if we knew it, is one with which we should be familiar. Who is he ?

On a street corner a few blocks above the hotel was standing a tall gentleman, somewhat past the prime of life, but of upright and military bearing, and wearing a long, sweeping mustache, slightly tinged with gray. His dark eyes and aquiline nose gave his countenance an aristocratic look. He seemed to be exploring his pockets for something, but, as the pedestrian approached, he stepped up to him, and said courteously :

" May I trouble you, sir, for a light for my cigar ? "

The other halted, took his cigar from his mouth, and handed it to the speaker with a bow. When the latter handed it back with a " Thank you ! " he remarked, " It's a cold evening," and passed on. Little did either imagine how soon and how strangely fate was to bring them together again.

The image of the military-looking gentleman passed into the other's memory, and remained there, never, so far as he knew, to be recalled. Continuing his brisk walk, he drew near one of the large club houses that decorate the avenue, just as a couple of men descended the steps arm-in-arm. One of them—a portly personage with a broad red beard—he recognized, and exchanged a silent salute with him; the other, a younger and slenderly built man, with small side-whiskers and a handsomely-cut mouth, was a stranger to him. "That's a clever fellow," he said to himself, as he strode onward. "A little cleverer than a club-man needs to be, I should imagine."

In a few minutes more, he turned down a side street, ran up the steps of a handsome house a short distance from the corner, and pulled the bell. The door was opened; he tossed away his cigar, and entered.

"Mr. Owens is at home?"

"He is, sir. Will you walk into the library?"

The visitor followed the servant down the wide and handsome hall, and passing through a door on the left found himself in a large room, the walls of which were lined with bookshelves to a height of five feet from the floor. The shelves were made of a light-colored wood, beautifully carved and polished, and were filled with books of various sizes, all in bindings that would have brought joy to the heart of a connoisseur of that rare and exquisite art. The walls above the bookcases were hung with stamped leather, enriched with a delicate design in gold, the tone of the whole being grateful to the eye, but not too dark. Standing upon the bookcases, in an apparently careless way, were framed engravings and etchings—proofs before lettering—many of the latter signed with the names of the artists, and having on their margins fanciful little designs, dashed off in idle moments during the pro-

gress of the main work. Dispersed around the room
—on brackets, on tables, in corners—was a unique
collection of bronzes, ancient and modern ; bronze
figures and groups, bronze vases, bronze lamps,
bronze caskets and ornaments — every thing in
bronze that was beautiful or quaint in form, masterly
in workmanship, and not larger than befitted the
size of the room. The ample fire-place, broader
than it was high, had a superb bronze mantelpiece,
designed by a Japanese artist, the supports being
two grotesque but solemn figures, half man and
half monster, the secret of whose creation is known
to the Japanese alone. Upon the tiled hearth
burned two or three great logs of cedar, the fragrance of whose burning pervaded the atmosphere.
The floor was made of polished oak, with rugs of
rich dull hues spread upon it here and there. The
room was lighted from a great globe of cream-
colored glass that descended from the ceiling like
some immense lustrous fruit hanging on a long
graceful stem. This light was very soft in quality,
yet was powerful enough to render the finest print
easily legible in the farthest corner of the
room.

But it would be impossible to paint an adequate
picture of this library, which is known to many
New Yorkers as beyond comparison the finest
owned by any private individual in the city. Both
the books and the bronzes were the rarest and most
finished specimens of their kind obtainable, and the
engravings and etchings were similarly unique.

Nothing in the room could have been exactly duplicated. It was the whim of the owner to render his library and its contents incomparable, and he had the means and resources to carry out his whim.

When the visitor entered the room, it was empty. The fire of cedar logs was blazing brightly on the hearth, whose polished surface reflected its light ; easy chairs and sofas extended to him a silent and luxurious invitation ; the rich and subdued hues of the books suggested solace to the mind ; the ornaments and decorations charmed the eye ; every thing combined to produce an impression of splendor softened into comfort. The room was no museum to be marveled at, but a retreat to be lived in—the home and haunt of a man in whose brain it had originated, and who knew how to use and appreciate it. It was organic and vital, not formal and lifeless. It gave evidence of the rich and cultivated intellect of which it was the material expression.

The visitor advanced to the fire-place, and stood there, drawing off his gloves, and examining the curious workmanship of a bronze clock that rested on the mantelpiece, when the sound of a step on the polished floor made him turn, and he saw the master of the house advancing to meet him.

" Glad to see you, Inspector Byrnes."

" How do you do, Mr. Owens ? "

Mr. Owens was evidently doing tolerably well. He was at this period a man of about thirty-five

years of age, with a handsome, intellectual countenance, clean-shaven mouth and chin, light brown
hair, thinning out on his high temples, and a figure and bearing that indicated clean living and
high breeding. Courtland Owen was the descen-
dant of several generations of American gentlemen ; he and his forefathers had been brought up
to wealth, and had taught themselves how to make a
graceful and fitting use of it. But, with the instinct of all genuine Americans, none of them had
been idle men. They had followed, some one av-
ocation, some another ; they had been merchants,
statesmen, diplomatists, bankers, directors of
great industrial enterprises ; all the higher offices
of citizenship had been filled by them with credit
and capacity. As for the present inheritor of the
name, he was first of all, by training and temperament, a student and a connoisseur : but he had
also entered into the active life of his day, and had
been for nearly ten years past the partner and personal friend of one of the greatest financiers of
the epoch. Never were two men more unlike than
the two members of this famous firm in every external appearance and characteristic ; and yet the
bond between them was much closer and more cordial than exists between many men far more at
one in general sympathies. They liked and respected each other as human beings, without reference to any thing else.

   " I have something I need your advice upon, Inspector," Mr. Owens remarked. "Take off your overcoat and sit down. I shan't let you go in five minutes, nor perhaps in half as many hours. So you might as well make yourself at home."

CHAPTER II.

A MODERN FINANCIER.

THE chief of the New York detectives, with the cheerful composure that belonged to him, removed his thick top-coat and seated himself near the hearth. Courtland Owens drew up a chair in proximity to his, and also within reach of a small inlaid table, containing a drawer fitted with a polished brass lock.

"We are in trouble," began Mr. Owens; "at least I am, on Golding's account."

"Golding—your partner! Why, what can be the matter with him?" The Inspector spoke with a certain sense of amusement; for Maxwell Golding, the man of mines, railroads, and telegraphs, whose riches were incalculable and whose luck in all enterprises was proverbial, seemed to the popular apprehension inaccessible to troubles, save such as might fall within the domain of the physician or, perhaps, the clergyman. But, as the Inspector glanced at his host's face, its serious expression apprised him that the matter could not be a light one; and he settled himself to listen to its unfolding with becoming gravity.

"I may as well tell you," the other went on, "that I am acting with Golding's consent, though I had some difficulty in obtaining it. You know the kind of man Golding is ; he is afraid of nothing. In his conduct of life he has practically eliminated the personal equation. He makes his way through all obstacles, to his point. Money is his instrument, but it is an instrument which no one knows how to use so boldly and effectively as himself. In fact, from his point of view money does not appear as dollars and cents ; it is the power to form combinations, to create values, to dissolve opposition. It is Prospero's magic wand ; only, instead of evoking illusions in a remote island, it brings into existence substantial realities all over a continent."

"But he has met with a check, has he?" demanded the inspector.

The other smiled. "I beg your pardon," said he. "You did not come here to talk philosophy and Shakespeare, and I had no business to digress upon them. Yes, Golding has met with a check, of a certain kind ; though he will not admit that he considers it one. It is easy to understand that a man like him would make enemies ; in fact, if he were a great deal more personally and promiscuously conciliating than he is, his enemies would still outnumber his friends as a hundred to one. It is a wonder he contrives to make any friends at all. To the vast number of his employés he is a sort of abstraction,—an embodiment of power and purpose directed to ends in which they are involved only incidentally, and from all concern with which — if they fail to do satisfactorily what is required of them—they are promptly dissociated. The wages that he pays them do not make them grateful ; for if they fulfill their duties, they regard their wages as only their just due ; and if they don't fulfill them, they are dismissed, and that's the end of it. So he can not look for friends among them. As for his rivals and competitors, so far as he may be said to have any, they are his enemies as a matter of course. He is more successful and powerful than they, and his loss would be their gain—at least, they imagine it would. He has ruined, or been the cause of the ruin, of many of them ; whether purposely or not I don't say, nor would it make any difference in the result. A man in his position is driven by fate ; he must either go forward or fall backward ; he can not remain at rest. Well, then, there remains another class,—the people who are employed neither by him nor his rivals. From them, if from any, his friends must come. But what chance has he of making friends among them ? It needs a bold man, and one exceptionally indifferent to criticism, to pose as the friend of a hundred-fold millionaire. His methods are suspected by every one, and, if he be a self-respecting man, he tells himself that the game is not worth the candle. If there were no other obstacle, however, there would still be the obstacle of Golding himself. A great capitalist is obliged to protect himself against idle intrusion, and he is easily suspicious of the disinterestedness of those who do approach him.   In short, there is almost no opportunity for him to form those ties that bind ordinary men together in the bonds of friendly good-fellowship.   For most practical intents and purposes he is—as Madame de Stael said Napoleon was—not a man, but a system.   His relations with the world are impersonal.   With the fewest possible exceptions, nobody knows him save by report, and nobody cares for him !"

" He's married, isn't he ?" inquired the Inspector.

" Fortunately, yes.   He met his wife while he was still a young man, and before there was any prospect of his attaining his unexampled position. He was assured of her affection before there was any reason to doubt its singleness and sincerity ; and his love for her and for their children is probably as strong as any passion in his nature—even as strong as his ambition.   Without the influence which his family has exerted over him, he might be as big a man as he is now, but he would have been a great deal more dangerous ; he would have had fewer scruples and less charity.   Even as it is, he is more cynical than a man ought to be, and his principles don't always agree with mine."

" But you are a friend of his, nevertheless."

" I am ; and I honestly believe he has no other. But my first acquaintance with him dates back to about the time of his marriage.   He had just sold that coal-mine that was located under his farm in Maryland, and had come up to New York to look about. Few people would have believed then that he had in him the making of the man he has since become, and yet he was just about the same looking sort of fellow that he is now,—rather short, rather broad, with black hair and a blue eye. It was only the eye that told the secret ; I never saw such an eye in a human head. Most of the time it has a sleepy appearance, as if the man was only half awake. But when any thing stirs him—when he is confronting an opposition or a peril that would scare any body else—then it gleams like fire ; a cold gleam, but it pierces right through you. There's something almost diabolical about it. He's a strange fellow."

" Still, you like him ? "

" Well, he has done some hard things—cruel things, perhaps ; but he has never done any thing that violates his own principles. He is a sort of Ishmael, starting out with the theory that no one is going to show him any mercy or consideration ; and he doesn't pretend to show any on his side. He meets cunning with cunning, and even duplicity with duplicity ; he is relentless so long as the fight continues, and he hesitates at no means short of crime to win it. But when the fight is over, he bears no malice, and takes no revenge. He is above feeling any personal enmity toward his rivals in business. He will shoulder them aside or tear them down, if they obstruct his designs ; but when their obstruction ceases, he is ready to give them the means to recover themselves. It sometimes seems to me as if Golding actually loves a dangerous antagonist; he enjoys the conflict even more than the victory; and when he has beaten his man in one battle, likes nothing better than to help him arm himself for another. Oh, yes, I like him!"

"I'm not surprised at such a man having enemies," observed the Inspector, after studying the blazing logs for a few moments. "What does surprise me is, that any of them should have the nerve to attack him. And yet, since you have called in my assistance, I infer that such is the fact?"

"And you are quite right. Yes, he would be a bold man who would openly and unaided defy Maxwell Golding. You know what money can buy in this city of New York; and Golding would not scruple to purchase any thing, from a watch-dog to a legislature, that would serve his ends. You know that as well as I do. But the peculiarity about this enemy is that, so far, Golding has been powerless to retaliate."

"How does that happen?"

"It is very simple. We don't know who he is."

"Anonymous, eh?" said the Inspector, sitting up in his chair. "How does he operate? Has he capital back of him? Do you feel him in the market?"

"Not at all. So far as it appears, it is quite the

other way. He is a man without any pecuniary
resources whatever."

" Then how does he continue to be offensive ? "

" There is always one way in which the weakest
man can make himself formidable to the strongest,
and that is by aiming at his life and that of those
who are dear to him. Walls of gold are no protection against the knife or bullet of an assassin. I
doubt if any capitalist, or syndicate of capitalists,
in this country, could bring down Golding ; but
any obscure blackguard who is desperate or crazy
enough to accept the consequences, may wipe him
out of existence at any moment by simply pressing
his finger against a trigger."

" Such vagabonds are not common," the Inspector remarked rather dryly.

" One would be enough," the other replied, " if
this should happen to be the one."

" Has Mr. Golding's life been attempted, then ? "

" It has been threatened, that is all."

" In that case," replied the Inspector, " I doubt
if there is any grave cause for anxiety. Threatened men live long. Of course, it is desirable to
put a stop to this thing, and I may be able to help
you do it ; but in case I succeed, Mr. Golding may
be under obligations to me for removing an annoy-
ance, but hardly for saving his life. The thing
stands to reason. If anybody really intends to
kill Mr. Golding, the last thing he would think of
doing would be to give him warning of it. He
would watch his opportunity, and strike, and that

would be both the beginning and the end of it. Barking dogs seldom bite."

"Very true, Inspector : but——"

"But if (as I gather from what you have told me) somebody is writing anonymous letters to Mr. Golding, announcing an intention of killing him, you may be pretty sure he will content himself with spilling ink ; blood is a touch beyond him."

"Granted, as a general rule," replied Mr. Owens, taking a small key from his pocket, and inserting it into the keyhole of the inlaid table. "But there is a class of men, as you must admit, whose actions do not square with ordinary rules or proprieties. They are not inspired by the motives that influence ordinary men."

"You mean——"

"I mean the class known as religious cranks."

"Oh !" ejaculated the Inspector, and paused. "Well," he continued, presently. "A genuine religious crank is a queer creature, and his proceedings are apt to be eccentric. But even he generally finds other ways of gratifying his eccentricities than by murder."

"Generally, perhaps. But you recollect what happened last summer in Washington ? "

"The assassination of Garfield. True. But Garfield was the President of the United States, and we do not know what political notions may have been behind that act."

"Politics makes fools of men, but religion

is more likely to drive them crazy," the other returned, " and then they become possessed with the
idea that it is their sacred mission to 'remove'
some conspicuous figure, be he President of the
United States, or its leading capitalist. It would not
be difficult for an unbalanced mind to persuade
itself that there were all the reasons in the deca-
logue for killing Golding—that he was a traitor to
his country, the corrupter of public morality, the
oppressor of the fatherless and the widow, anti-
christ, Lucifer, and all the rest of it. That is all
he needs for a motive. As to his giving his intended victim warning of what to expect,
that may be unwise ; but it doesn't seem to me,
under the circumstances, unnatural. He wishes to
define his position as a God-inspired avenger of
iniquity. He desires to kill the body but not the
soul ; he will give his victim opportunity to say
his prayers and make his will, or, on the other
hand, if he is animated by a personal hatred, and
is not satisfied to inflict the momentary agony of
the death-blow, what more effective torment can
he devise than that of suspense—the Sword of
Damocles ! However, you shall judge for yourself."

With these words Mr. Owens turned the key in
the lock of the inlaid table, and opened the drawer.

CHAPTER III.

A BUNDLE OF LETTERS.

FROM the drawer Mr. Owens took a packet of letters, inclosed in an elastic band, and handed them to the Inspector.

"As you will see by the postmarks," he observed, "they have been coming during the last three weeks or thereabouts. For a time, Golding paid no attention to them, beyond directing his secretary to keep them. He has been threatened, anonymously and otherwise, before ; and you are probably aware that there has occasionally been a strong popular feeling against him in the city. But he is something of a fatalist, and takes every thing very coolly, as I said. I suppose if a bomb were to explode behind his chair, and blow a hole through the floor of his office, he would hardly trouble himself to turn round. It was only by accident that he mentioned the affair to me at all. I was asking after his wife's health—she had been a little indisposed—and he said that her nerves had been upset by the last letter she received. I asked what he meant, and he finally showed me the collection."

"Has he, or any one, taken any measures to discover the writer?"

"None whatever. Golding thought he might betray himself after a while, and did not consider it worth the trouble of an investigation. If it had not been for his wife, I fancy he would have refused to act entirely. But it began to have an effect on her health, not so much because she herself was threatened, as because she feared for him. After seeing the letters, I advised him to have something done at once. He laughed, and pooh-poohed the suggestion; but finally he yielded. That was this morning; and I sent down for you immediately."

The Inspector removed the elastic band from the letters, and glanced at the superscriptions. There were upwards of half-a-dozen envelopes, all addressed to either Mr. or Mrs. Maxwell Golding. The chirography was the same in all,—a compact, small, irregular hand, as if the writer had either attempted to disguise his own style, or was an awkward and unpracticed penman. Paper and envelopes were of the same size and quality, cheap and ordinary; the postmark showed that they had all been posted in New York city. The letters were without date or name. Any one of the million inhabitants of the metropolis might have written them, so far as their external appearance was concerned.

"I'll begin at the beginning," said the Inspector: and he unfolded the first letter, which was as follows:—

"Maxwell Golding—Sir: You must prepare to

leave this world, in which you have done so much
wickedness. Your hour is at hand. Your contemptible race is run. You may think yourself great
and powerful, one of the mighty of the earth ; but
you are mortal and you are now to die. Make your
peace with God if you can, for He has commanded
me to kill you—to shoot you down like a dog.   I
am the chosen instrument of His Providence.   The
Lord giveth and the Lord taketh away.   He gave
you your riches, but you have misused it, and now,
by my hand, He is going to take away your worthless and wicked life.   I must do His bidding, and
I shall smite and spare not ; but I am willing to
give you time to prepare your immortal soul for the
awful change.   Probably your wife and children
will have to die also ; but I am not yet convinced
whether the Lord requires this or not.   It is better
that you be cut off root and branch.   I shall write
to you once more, and then you will not hear from
me again till you lie weltering in your blood at my
feet.   I long to be at the Lord's work, but I will
spare you yet a few days. All men will applaud and
justify the deed.   I shall be called a hero and a
liberator.   But I desire no glory for myself—only to
kill you, as the Lord commands.   Blessed be the
name of the Lord.   Say good-by to your wife and
children, and settle your affairs, for I swear before
God that you will be a corpse in a few days."

    " How does it strike you ? " asked Mr. Owens, as
the Inspector folded up the letter and replaced it
in its envelope.

" Well, it isn't the sort of thing to give a man an appetite for his breakfast," the other returned. " But I don't think—judging off-hand—that it is a genuine letter. It has a false ring to it. It reads more as if the fellow were trying to imitate what he supposed a religious crank would write than like a real religious crank's writing. Of course I may be mistaken."

" But what can be his object—supposing him to be an impostor ? "

" Oh, it would be object enough to scare Mr. Golding. There is a great deal of merely idle mischievousness in the world. But I take it he has an object—a real and practical one—though it doesn't appear in that letter."

" What do you mean ? "

" I mean that I think he wants to extort money."

" Why doesn't he say so then ? "

" Perhaps he will later on. He is proceeding methodically. This letter tells Mr. Golding that he will be a corpse in a few days ; and yet it was written over three weeks ago, and Mr. Golding is not a corpse yet. That is suspicious."

" Well, look at the other letters," said Mr. Owens.

The Inspector resumed his examination, and during an interval of fifteen minutes there was no sound in the library except the crackling of the logs on the hearth, and the low ticking of the bronze clock on the mantelpiece. The detective did not simply read the letters ; he investigated them in the minutest detail. He compared words as written in one with the same word in the others. He noted the kind of ink used, and the pattern of pen that had probably been employed. He contrasted the purport of one letter with that of the rest, weighing the phrases and expressions, and striving to penetrate beneath their literal form to the mind and character of the writer. He considered the grammar and the style of composition, to determine whether the author were an uneducated man trying to appear educated, or an educated man trying to appear ignorant. At length he replaced all the letters in the elastic band, and put the packet on the table.

"Have you modified your opinion?" Mr. Owens inquired.

"In some respects I have," replied the other, slowly. "In the first place, I think those letters were written by a man of culture—by what would be called a gentleman."

"I have come to the opposite conclusion. Leaving the handwriting aside, a gentleman, or one holding that position, would not use language so crude and awkward."

"Not if he were writing, so to say, in his own person; but he is acting a part. He is a clever, wide-awake man-of-the-world, studying to appear like a half-crazed religious enthusiast. The assumption is very well done; but there are lapses here and there; there are some sentences, and especially some ideas, in the letters that the kind of man he is aping would never use or think of. And apart from that, there is too much self-consciousness throughout."

" You may be right ; but admitting that you are, what difference would it make ? Golding might be shot by an educated man just as well as by a day laborer."

" Not if the educated man is disguising his true character."

" Why not ? "

" Because there must be a reason for that disguise. If this fellow really meant to kill Golding, he might conceal his name, but what object could he have in trying to make it appear that he belonged to another rank in life than his real one ? That would not bring him any nearer to his end. If Golding is to be murdered, it is all one to him who fires the shot. I say, therefore, that the intention is not murder, but something else."

" Money ? "

" Exactly. He means first to frighten his man, and then to work upon his fears for pecuniary purposes. You observe how he postpones the day of execution, on one point or another, again and again. The pretexts are ingeniously devised, but not ingeniously enough to conceal the ingenuity. He is holding something in reserve ; and before long, unless I am much mistaken, he will spring it upon him. He will demand money as the condition of sparing Golding's life—money, or the means of getting it."

" That is to say, inside information about the market."

" Precisely. Now, I observe another thing about this fellow. In some way or another, he has very accurate information as to Golding's movements and habits. One would say he must stand in tolerably intimate relations with him. In fact, he says as much in the letter—that he is able, at any moment in the day, to accomplish the assassination."

" Yes ; I noticed that myself."

" Of course, it may be open to a slightly different interpretation. He may merely have acquired certain information about Golding, in order, by appearing to be in a position to gain immediate access to him, to frighten him the more thoroughly. It would certainly add to a threatened man's uneasiness to believe that his secret enemy was some intimate personal acquaintance—perhaps his confidential secretary, or some business colleague. He would feel no security anywhere, even in the bosom of his own family."

" Like the Czar of Russia, who finds messages from the Nihilists in his napkin at the breakfast-table, or under his pillow at night."

" But I am inclined to think, at present, that the writer really does know Golding, and gets his information about him at first hand. And I think so the more, because it would be to the advantage of the writer that I should think otherwise."

" I don't quite follow you."

" What I mean is this. These letters were written for my benefit, as well as for Mr. Golding's. The writer saw that they would sooner or later be submitted to me, and he therefore attempts to mislead me as well as him. He argued that I would infer, from certain indirect evidence in the letters, that he was personally acquainted with Golding; so, in order to head me off from that conclusion, he declares in so many words that he is acquainted with him."

" I understand! He anticipates that you will believe him a liar, and therefore he tells the exact truth."

" In this instance—yes. Well, you see the corollary? If he stands so near Golding, it can not be so difficult to pick him out. The field of selection is immensely narrowed. From hundreds of thousands, say, we come down at one step to tens or twenties."

Mr. Owens looked at the detective curiously. " You certainly deserve your reputation, Inspector," he said thoughtfully.

The other smiled. " Wait till we are out of the woods!" he said. " And to that end, I may as well ask you a question or two. Looking at the matter in the light we now have upon it, is there any one you would feel inclined to suspect?"

Owens shook his head slowly. "I haven't thought of any one."

" You know all the people who are likely to be about Golding?"

" Yes, I suppose I do."

" Well, is there any one of those men whom Golding has at any time injured, or quarreled with, or by any means made his enemy ? "

Owens took his chin between his thumb and fore-finger, and reflected.

" The men who work with Golding, or for him, are apt to be wholly devoted to his interests," he said after a while. " They may not like him, as one man likes another, but they admire him, and will do any thing for him. They are like soldiers towards their general ; he may be a martinet or a tyrant, but he inspires enthusiasm and commands obedience, because they feel that he knows what he is about, and the best way to go to work. Golding might act very severely or harshly towards his subordinates or associates, and yet they might never think of turning against him. At all events, I doubt if I could throw any light in that direction. Any one of them will be just as likely or unlikely to feel a grudge as any other."

" Is there no one who has formerly been on friendly terms with him, but who, for any reason, has since broken with him, either openly or covertly ? "

Owens began to shake his head, but all at once a thought seemed to strike him ; he bit his lips, looked grave, and finally said with a smile :

" Well, it has just occurred to me that there is a man who fits that description very well. But he is not the man we are after."

" How do you know he is not ? "

" Oh, it is impossible ! There isn't a more honorable man in New York, or one with a higher business reputation. He's really quite out of the question."

The detective looked his interlocutor steadily in the face.

" Mr. Owens," he said, " in an affair of this kind there is no one who can be beyond suspicion. The more extreme the improbability seems to be, the more reason may exist for an investigation. An anonymous letter may come from the person whom you consider to be your dearest friend ; it may come from the deacon of your church, or the president of your bank. I tell you frankly, Mr. Owens, that for all I know, you may have written those letters yourself."

" Well, I didn't ! " said the other, laughing.

" I am quite in earnest in saying," continued the detective, "that although it may be impossible to find out who did write the letters, it is certainly impossible to attest beforehand that any particular person did not. I am here, at your request, to do my utmost to discover the writer. If you wish me to succeed, the least you can do is to give me the names of all persons known to you who are physically capable of having written them. For you to do this does not imply that you believe in the guilt of any of those persons. But if you wish to clear them of suspicion, the only way is to let me investigate them."

"Very well, Inspector," said Mr. Owens good humoredly, rising from his chair and standing with his back to the fire. "I'll tell you the name of the man I am thinking of, and on your head be it! Did you ever hear of Gilbert Cowran?"

CHAPTER IV.

"GILBERT COWRAN?" repeated the detective, looking up. "Do you refer to the lawyer of that name?"

"That is the man I mean."

There was a short silence. Inspector Byrnes leaned back in his chair and gazed thoughtfully at the cornice. Owens turned round and gave one of the logs a kick with his foot. Then he faced about again.

"You see the absurdity of the thing now, I presume," he said.

The detective made no direct answer to this remark.

"I know Mr. Cowran by name and reputation," he said, "and I have occasionally seen him in court. But I know nothing about his relations with Mr. Golding. They were friends, you say, and afterwards quarreled?"

"The story is no secret, and I have no objection to telling it. Golding's connection with Cowran was formed soon after Golding's arrival in New York. Cowran, at that time, was little known; he was a young fellow of ability and promise in his profession, but his clients were not many and his means were not great. Golding happened to run across him at a time he was looking for some one to defend a suit. He saw that Cowran was a fit man for the business, and retained him. That affair led to others. Golding got in the habit of consulting Cowran on all legal matters. The two soon took a fancy to each other. In a few years, Cowran was Golding's confidential agent and adviser. His connection with Golding had profited him professionally. Besides the money he received for managing Golding's affairs, he acquired a large and valuable general practice. His remarkable talents were recognized, and he had a great future before him. There was a time when he could have had the District-Attorneyship if he had cared for it. I think Golding wanted him to take it ; but Cowran's ambition didn't lie in the direction of politics : and besides, the regular practice of his profession brought him in a larger income than the legitimate proceeds of a municipal office.

" Things went on in that way until the period of the great panic on Wall Street, a few years ago. Cowran was at that time making a great deal of money every year, though I don't suppose he had laid up any large capital. He was always inclined to be liberal and expensive in his habits. As for Golding, he was already then, as he is now, the heaviest and most formidable man on the street.

" Nobody but Golding and Cowran know the

whole inside history of that affair. I never asked Golding about it, or Cowran either, for I was a friend of both parties. But what appeared to out-siders was something like this—Golding was interested in a certain stock, and had secretly arranged to get control of it. He consulted with Cowran as to the best means of doing this, Cowran advising him, of course, from the legal point of view ; for Cowran is not much of a financier. But, naturally, he knew what Golding meant to do.

" I don't believe he had ever speculated, in the full sense of the word, before. I don't know what put it into his head to do so on the present occa-sion. Perhaps he had a special need for money, and thought he had a sure thing. Whether or not he told Golding what he was going to do, I can't say. At all events, he went in very heavily, and kept on increasing his investments, confidently expecting the promised change in the market. Before long he had put in about every thing he possessed.

" But meanwhile Golding, for some reason or other, had altered his plans. He made up his mind to drop the stock that he had intended to boom. Of course he must have neglected to inform Cow-ran of this change. That was the ground of the quarrel between them, as I understood it. It is quite possible, however, that Golding did not know that Cowran had been speculating, or he may have been unable, for business reasons, to fore-warn even him of the new deal. Those are ques-tions that may never be settled. I can only say that

it is, on the face of it, unlikely that he devised
Cowran's ruin.   There is nothing to show that he
could in any way have served his interests.   On
the contrary, he might easily have injured them.
Be that as it may, when the crash came, Cowran
was landed high and dry.   It was a very bad case.
When all his liabilities were paid, he had scarcely
a thousand dollars cash left.

   " He and Golding had an interview ; no third
person was present, but I fancy it was pretty violent.   Cowran has a fierce temper, and Golding,
on such occasions, is cold and hard as steel.   They
parted in anger, and have had no communication
with each other since.   But though they are enemies, they are honorable in their enmity.   Cowran preserves, among his office papers, records of
transactions which, if he were to make them public,
would seriously affect some of Golding's interests.
But he has never made any use of them.   Golding,
on the other hand, could have put insurmountable
obstacles in the way of Cowran's recovering from
his disaster, but I am inclined to think that he did
just the opposite.   Very few people ever knew that
Cowran had lost money.   He immediately sold his
house and hired rooms in a cheap flat.   He kept
his office down town, and by great effort succeeded
in paying the rent of it.   He set to work, with
the courage and determination that are characteristic of him, to build himself up again.   But it
proved to be a longer and harder work than it had
been before.   There was more competition, for

one thing ; and the loss of Golding's business meant many thousands a year. Nevertheless, he has done well, and his reputation, personal and professional, is as high as ever. I have always looked forward to bringing the two men together again and getting up a reconciliation between them. I certainly don't anticipate that Cowran can so far have changed his nature and character as to put on the guise of a secret assassin, and I expect that your investigations, if you make any, will lead you to the same conclusion."

" So far as your story tells me any thing, I would be disposed to share your expectation," Inspector Byrnes replied. " But you say, yourself, that you do not know the inside of the affair ; and something may have occurred that would arouse a more deadly animosity on Cowran's part than the mere loss of his fortune would do. No man ever thoroughly knows another ; one sometimes sees very strange developments in human nature. By the way, there is one very important request that I have to make of you."

" What is that ? "

" It is that you make no mention whatever to Cowran of what has occurred between us. It might destroy the whole case."

" I will agree to that," said the other ; " I promise you that I won't open my mouth on the subject, to him or any one else."

" Thank you. Secrecy, as you are aware, is an essential condition of the success of all detective operations. It should not even be known that any detective operations are contemplated. You had better let no one suspect that you have so much as received a call from me."

" I appreciate the precaution, and shall observe it. But can I not afford you any more positive help than simply to hold my tongue ? "

" No help is more useful, and there is none that we get less of than silence," the detective replied : " If you give us that, you will have done your fair share. But if there is any other person that you can think of—"

Mr. Owens shook his head.

" I don't admit that I suspect Cowran," he said. " I can certainly name no other."

"Mr. Golding, I think you said, is happy in his domestic relations ? "

" Entirely so."

" There is no chance of his having been led to make any connection which—"

" My dear Inspector, don't think of such a thing ! I doubt if Golding has so much as spoken to a dozen women in his life. His habits are as regular as clock-work. He goes from his home to his office, and from his office work to his home. He neither drinks nor smokes. He is actually an ascetic. I should as soon suspect Saint Simeon Stylites of making an irregular connection as of his doing so."

" You must remember," the Inspector remarked, " that you are the only person to whom I can apply for information. All the other evidence that I obtain must be extracted without any knowledge, on the part of those who give it, of the object of the inquiries. If any thing were to leak out, there is no telling who might give the alarm. I shall be assisted in this investigation by only one detective,—a young man in whose ability and discretion I place much confidence. But as things stand now, I am bound to tell you that the outlook is not very promising."

" It certainly appears rather dark."

" In fact, if the writer of the letters be really a religious crank, we may have to trust more to the chapter of accidents than to any thing else, to discover who he is. Such men do not answer decoy advertisements, or fall into any of the traps that catch ordinary rogues. But if personal enmity or personal gain enters into the calculations of an unknown friend, the odds will be in our favor."

"I hope on all accounts that such will prove to be the case."

"One of my first acts will be to attempt to determine that point. Meanwhile I shall depend on you to keep me informed of any further developments in the matter."

" All future letters that may be received will be sent direct to me at my office. I will attend to that personally." After a pause he added, " Of course, if any thing should by any chance appear against Cowran, I presume the matter could be arranged without publicity. I have not Golding's authority to say so, of course, for the suggestion will be as strange to him as it was to me, but I think that will be his feeling."

"I am an officer," answered the Inspector. "When I have identified the writer, my interest in the affair will cease."

"You said you knew Cowran, didn't you?"

"By sight—slightly. He is a member of the American League Club, isn't he?"

"Yes. He is on the Council, I believe."

"I saw him coming out of the Club as I was on my way here,—a big sturdy fellow with a red beard."

"His personal appearance is certainly not against him."

"There was a young fellow with him, whom I didn't recognize,—short side-whiskers, good-looking, rather in the English style."

"Probably Frank Cunliffe. It sounds like him."

"Has he any particular relations with Cowran?"

"Not that I know of. They are both members of the Club, that's all."

"He doesn't know Mr. Golding, I suppose?"

"Who, Cunliffe? Not at all. He is just a young fellow about town; I know nothing of him, good or bad. Certainly nothing bad."

"If I ever have a biographer, I hope it may be such a man as you are," said the Inspector, taking up his overcoat with a smile. "It isn't every body that takes such a hopeful view of human nature as you do."

" I speak of it as I find it. Why not ? "

" Well, you would never be able to pass your apprenticeship in my business. The Good Book says that charity covereth a multitude of sins. My business is to uncover sins ; so I am obliged to be economical with my charity."

" And yet," said the other, giving another kick to the cedar log, which fell apart and sent a shower of bright sparks careering up the chimney, " your charity may be of a sounder quality than mine. Mine is chiefly a matter of temperament ; I like to have a good opinion of people, because it would be unpleasant to think evil of them. You test every thing, and when you find gold it is gold and no mistake."

" Perhaps that is the reason I meet with so little consideration at my banker's," the Inspector returned ; and with a laugh and a shake of the hand the two men parted.

CHAPTER V.

THE next day an advertisement to the following effect appeared in the columns of one of the New York journals :

" The instrument of Divine Vengeance. Can M. G. communicate with you ? any method you suggest will be strictly observed. Do not commit an injustice. The Lord giveth and the Lord taketh away. Answer by letter."

This advertisement was continued for a week.

The American League Club is one of the largest, and at the same time is held to be one of the most exclusive, in New York. It certainly numbers among its members some of the wealthiest and most respectable men in the city. It occupies a stately and somewhat gloomy building on one of the avenues : its habitués maintain an august decorum, and never get into the newspapers unless they want to. They do not appear to be especially gregarious ; they roam about the great rooms by ones and twos, seldom by threes, and four together would be considered a crowd, and hardly good form. Probably no man in the club would even pretend to know by sight so many as a tenth part of those whose names appear upon the roll. At certain fixed intervals during the year the club holds receptions, which are largely attended, and at seasons of political storms or emergency meetings are called and resolutions are passed,—for the club piques itself upon its weight in political affairs. The club is also a patron of art, and there is an annual exhibition of paintings by American artists in its rooms. Upon the whole, it may be considered a model club, and as such its members are fond of showing it to their foreign guests, especially to those from the mother country, and asking them how it compares with the famous palaces on St. James Street and Pall Mall.

Among the latest of the English guests introduced to the club, at the period of which we write, was a gentleman known as Captain Raleigh Hamilton. He was understood to be a relative of the renowned English explorer whose death or disappearance on the upper Nile was one of the sensations of Christendom. But aside from this distinguished connection—to which, by the way, the Captain betrayed a modest indisposition to allude— he was voted to be a capital fellow. His manner had a military punctiliousness and courtesy which nevertheless did not disguise the genial and social qualities beneath. He was polished, well-read and well-informed ; he had been everywhere and seen every thing : like his great cousin he had been something of a free-lance, having improved his

leisure by fighting under the banners of several
nations ; yet he was by no means given to rehears-
ing the story of his campaigns, and was, indeed,
rather noted for his reticence under circumstances
when many men would have waxed loquacious
and boastful. Captain Hamilton played a fair
game of billiards, though the small American
tables, with their three balls and no pockets, perplexed him a little at first, but at whist he was as
good as the best, and he exhibited symptoms of
an ability to become proficient, some day, at poker.
He was by no means a gambler, however, but uni-
formly refused to play for high stakes, remarking,
with the frank simplicity that belonged to him,
that he couldn't afford it. Like all clubbable
Englishmen, he was fond of keeping behind the
club windows, and could very seldom be induced
to go out in society, alleging that women always
made him stupid. Like all Englishmen, also, he
was fond of horses, and confessed to a special interest in the American trotter. Perceiving this such of
his entertainers as owned trotters competed for the
pleasure of taking the Captain for a spin in the
park, and regaling him, not with the diversion alone,
but with startling statistics of what the kings and
queens of the American track had done or could do
when they were really put to it.

Among the first of the members of the club with
whom Captain Hamilton showed a disposition to
make more than a passing acquaintance, was Gilbert Cowran. He remarked that Cowran looked

like a Scot, and was delighted to learn that he had Scotch blood in him. "We Hamiltons are Scotch, you know," he observed. "I was pretty sure, from the cut of your jib, that you or your people must have come from north of the Tweed."

"My father was born in Edinbro," Cowran replied. "He emigrated in 1849, and settled in New Jersey, where a good many of his countrymen live."

"Were you educated in the old country?" inquired Hamilton.

"No, I have never been back. I was sent to Columbia, and studied law there after taking my degree. I have been here pretty much ever since."

"Well, you lawyers are better off than we army fellows. You always have something to do. Some of the barristers and Q. C.'s in London get awfully rich. But I suppose you make more here than they do there."

"I don't know about that. If I'm a fair example, I should say no."

"I fancy a fellow spends more here than he does in London."

"Possibly. At any rate, he loses more, I guess, if he's fool enough to back the wrong side to win."

"You mean horses."

"No, I was thinking of Wall Street."

"Oh, I've heard about that. I must get down there some day and have a look at 'em. I wonder if some fellow will give me a point!"

" Judging from my own experience, I should say several persons would be very glad to do so," Cowran replied, rather grimly. " What would be the result to you is another question."

" Oh, I'm not altogether an ass in money matters, you know," said the Captain, pleasantly. " I can't afford to throw money away, as I have said before ; but I have a few thousands that I wouldn't mind putting out to advantage, and from what I hear it would be easy to double or treble it in a few weeks, if a fellow got hold of the right stock."

" Well, you will do as you like, of course ; it's none of my affair. Only, I should be sorry to have you plucked while you are the guest of the club."

" Oh, come now ! It isn't as bad as that, surely ? Of course I suppose there are sharpers on the street, as there are everywhere ; but I'm speaking of the really solid fellows, who control every thing —persons like Golding and Vanderwick. I don't fancy there'd be any danger in following the advice of Golding, now, for instance ?"

" Maxwell Golding is a clever man," returned Cowran, putting an egg in his egg-cup and cracking the top of it with his spoon,—the two were breakfasting together. " He is a clever man ; I might almost say a great man, if a man whose whole soul is in finance can properly be called great. He is a master of his art, and performs with a turn of his finger marvels that would make Monte Cristo look like a fool, and give Aladdin a headache." Here he dropped a pinch of salt into his egg. " He is as powerful a man as there is in this country to-day. Russia is a despotism, but she has only one Czar, and he has the Nihilists against him; but," continued Cowran, his voice deepening, "America is a republic, and has a thousand despots, and Maxwell Golding is the chief of them! What is there he can not do or buy? His creed is that every man has his price; or if his price can't be found, he can be crushed. Golding is above the law; if the laws that exist don't suit him, he breaks them: if it is too much trouble to break them, he gets other laws passed for his convenience. The legislators, the judges, the lawyers *pro* and *con*, the juries, the newspapers, all belong to him. The public is a helpless fool; he knows it, and wouldn't mind saying it. His enemies he annihilates as a matter of course; that's only what might be expected; but his friends suffer even more. He leads them on until they feel secure, and believe that he values their interests equally with his own; and then he cuts them down and roots them up and sows the place in which they flourished with salt. Talk about sharpers! Take your money—all you have—and have it paid to you in gold coin by the bank. Carry it to the worst slum in the city, and pile it up on the sidewalk. Leave it there all day and all night, and go back to look for it in the morning. Do you think you would find it intact?"

"Well, hardly!"

"Then I tell you, and I know what I am talking

about, that the chances would be ten times as great
in favor of finding every dollar where you left it,
as if you followed Golding's friendly advice as to
investing in his stocks.   He wouldn't be satisfied
with taking all you had ; he would get a mortgage
on every thing you could ever hope to make hereafter.   And you would be powerless to retaliate.
All would have been done correctly, according to
the rules of the street !   I sometimes think that
perhaps a little Nihilism wouldn't be a bad thing
in New York.   A bomb would do more to bring
such fellows to reason than all the law in the
country."

"Oh, I say, Cowran ! You're not in earnest, you
know.   A fellow may hate a man without wanting
to blow him up, by Jove !"

Cowran's eyes were sparkling, and his face was
flushed but he controlled himself by an effort.   "I
am speaking in the abstract, of course," he said
presently.   "But it is a truth which the history of all
oppression confirms, that, when legitimate means
fail to punish high-handed wrong, men will take
the law into their own hands, and Golding is as
likely as any other to be forced to realize that truth
in his own case."

"Well, I'd no notion it was as bad as that over
here," the captain remarked cl eerfully.   "One
always has the idea that every bod has a good time
in America, and makes lots of mon y.   As for this
man Golding—you say you speak in the abstract—

you mean you don't know him personally, I suppose ?"

"I have had nothing to do with him for several years ; I have nothing to say as to what relations we may have had in the past. My story would be only a little more ugly than that of a hundred others. Pshaw ! it isn't worth while to let one's breakfast get cold for such a matter. All I wanted was to give you an idea of what you are to expect down there among the bulls and bears."

"Well, I've been in some pretty lively scrimmages in my time," said the captain, toying with his coffee-cup, "and I've shot tigers in India, and all that sort of thing ; but I fancy I wouldn't make much of a show among your bulls and bears, after all. And I'm much obliged to you, my dear Cowran, for putting me up to the game."

Cowran nodded, but made no reply ; and the captain, turning his chair and crossing his legs, took up a paper and began to glance idly up and down its columns, refreshing himself meanwhile with occasional swallows of coffee.

Presently he laid the paper on his knee, and turned to his companion.

"I've often thought," he said, "what a deuced entertaining book it would make if some fellow was to get a lot of the ' personals ' in the newspapers, and put 'em together—connecting all those that seemed to have been written by the same people, you know. It might be possible, in that way, to find out what they were writing about. Some of

them read as if there might be some very odd
stories behind 'em. Do you ever look at 'em ?"

" Once in a while, I suppose. I never gave any
thought to the matter. Are there any interesting
ones this morning ?"

" I don't know ; nothing particular. This one
at the top of the column is as good as any. ' The
Instrument of Divine Vengeance,' it begins. That's
some formula, probably, by which the person it's
addressed to is to recognize the writer. ' Can M.
G. communicate with you ? Any method you suggest will be strictly observed. Do not commit an
injustice.' There's a suggestion to follow up, you
see ! ' The Lord giveth and the Lord taketh
away.' This fellow seems to be a sort of religious
crank.—' Answer by letter.' That's all there is of
it. Who's ' M. G.' do you suppose ?"

" ' M. G.' ? Humph ! That's curious ! Let me
look at it," said Cowran, taking the paper. He
read the paragraph, and fell into a brown study
over it, pulling his great red beard, and drawing
his brows together. At length he roused himself,
and handed the paper back.

" Well, do you make out who ' M. G.' is ?" demanded the captain, with a smile.

" Who, I ? No, how should I ? Some woman,
very likely. It set me thinking about something,
that's all."

" Try one of these cigars," said the captain.

CHAPTER VI.

NEWS.

LATE on the afternoon of the next day, a handsome sleigh found its way to Mulberry Street, and drew up in front of a large building with a white stone facing, over the doorway of which was an inscription signifying that this was the headquarters of the Metropolitan Police. A gentleman in a fur-lined overcoat alighted from the sleigh and ran up the steps and asked the doorkeeper the way to the Detective Bureau.

The doorkeeper indicated an entrance on the left, and the visitor was conducted through a series of rooms and corridors and wicker gates and behind wire screens, until he reached a small anteroom with a desk and chair in it ; here there was a moment's pause, and then he was ushered into a handsome sitting-room, and Inspector Byrnes advanced to meet him with outstretched hand.

" Glad to see you so soon again, Mr. Owens," he said. " But you're not come on business, are you ? There can't have any thing new happened yet ? "

" I expect you know nearly as much about that

as I do," the other replied, throwing open his overcoat and taking a chair. " Things certainly begin to move in a remarkable manner as soon as you take hold of them. That ' personal ' of yours was very cleverly worded."

" You don't mean to say that any thing has come of it ? "

" There has, though ! Our anonymous friend seems to be a reader of that paper. I came right here from my office, so as to lose no time."

" Have you learned any thing about him ? "

" Golding has received a letter from him, referring to the ' personal.' "

" Well, that is something, after all. What does he say ? "

" I have brought the letter with me. Here it is," and he took an envelope from his pocket and handed it to the Inspector.

The latter opened it and read the words that follow :—

" M. Golding. Sir :—I have seen in a paper, accidentally, a paragraph which bears your initials, and seems to have some reference to the mission of destruction with which the Lord has charged me towards you. If you expect, by any such devices, to discover who I am, you are much mistaken. Though you see me every day, and I know all your movements, you will never recognize me as the avenger of Providence until you feel the blow that will send you from this world forever. If you think that you can offer me any inducements to spare you, you are equally wrong. I know you are wealthy, and you may think that, because I am poor, you can buy me off. But you need not flatter yourself. Your doom is written ; and even if I, for any reason, did not execute it, the Lord would raise up some other instrument of His purpose. If I had wanted money, I should have spoken of it before this. But I have told you the simple facts ; I had no other meaning, and my wife and family will gladly starve rather than that I should falter in my sacred mission. Prepare your soul for eternity, for the time is now ripe, and I am weary of delay. If you have any last requests to make you may put them in the same newspaper. I am willing to grant you any favor that does not conflict with my immovable purpose."

The Inspector folded up the letter and burst into a saturnine laugh.

" Well, that is pretty plain talking, between business men, isn't it ? " he said.

" You think he will consent to a parley, then ? "

" Consent to a parley ! Why, you can hear the jingle of coin in every word ! We said nothing in our ' personal ' about money, that I know of. He has put the words into our mouth. He is even more avaricious than I gave him credit for. And yet the letter is shrewd enough, too. He sticks to his religious lingo, and talks about being weary of delay. Yes, it isn't a bad piece of work."

" But you are convinced that money is what he wants ? "

" As much as I am convinced that a fish wants water."

" And that his only object has been to frighten Golding into treating with him ? "

" And he fancies that he has succeeded in doing it. Meanwhile, you can assure Mr. Golding that if his life depended on this man's actions he would live to a hundred. Not only that, but if his life were in any danger, this man would risk his own to save him. He is not going either to kill the goose that lays the golden eggs himself or allow any one else to do it. He is a blackmailer, and that is all there is about it."

" But blackmailers are never satisfied. If we were to give him money, he would come back for more, and so on indefinitely."

" There is no doubt about that. And yet the only way to put an end to the nuisance will be to give him money, or rather to let him make some, and perhaps a good deal of it."

" But that will not put an end to the nuisance permanently."

" It will, unless he is a cleverer rogue than the majority of his kind."

" I don't catch your idea."

" Well, leaving details out for the present, this is the idea in a nutshell : If you give him money, and he receives it, you will have a clue to catch him by. He must either go to get the money himself, or send some one to get it for him ; and then it will be my fault if he is not detected."

" But if he is as clever as you say, he will see that danger himself."

" A man's desires, if they are strong enough, always obscure his judgment. He will suggest some means of transacting the affair which he will consider safe. It may not occur to him that you have put the matter in my hands ; at all events he will have to risk something in order to gain his end. Now that I know the sort of man I am dealing with, the worst of the difficulty is over."

" How shall you answer this letter ? "

For answer, the Inspector took a sheet of paper and a pen, and after meditating for a few moments began to write. When the writing was finished, he passed it over to his visitor.

Its purport was to this effect :—" The instrument of the Lord's vengeance.—M. G. acknowledges that a doom which is written can not be escaped. You have produced a deep impression upon him. He wishes, if possible, to make reparation for some of the evil he may have done. Can nothing be arranged for your wife and family ? Can you devise a plan by which he can communicate with you through this column ? You misinterpret the motive of his former advertisement. Write freely, and your wishes will be attended to. He only asks that you reveal the secret to no one."

" I can suggest no improvement," said Mr. Owens, after reading it. " That touch about the wife and children is admirable."

" It is a mere formality. He can read between

my lines as easily as I can read between his ; but
it is just like many observances in social life ; every
body knows that they are humbug, but they are
observed just the same. We may venture on plainer
talk by and by. We will keep up the religious
pretense as long as he does ; and I'll make bold
to prophesy that that won't be very long."

While this conversation was going on at the Central office, Gilbert Cowran was seated in his place
of business down town, writing letters. All the
clerks had gone home but one, for it was after
hours ; this one was in Cowran's confidence, and
had been in his employ for several years. He was
busy looking up some references for an argument.

"Talbot," said Cowran, after sealing and ad-
dressing his last letter.

"Yes, Mr. Cowran," said Talbot, looking up.

"Do you recollect that last suit that we defended
for Golding? It was soon after that big deal of
his, you know."

"I think I do, sir. He was sued for willful mis-
representation, or something of that kind, the
plaintiff's object being to force him to reveal the
secret history of his operation in open court. He
communicated with you and sent his private papers
and memoranda relating to the operation in question to you, in order that you might be able to
judge of the best line of defense. You arranged
that——"

"Yes, that's all right. What I wanted to ask you

was, whether those papers and memoranda are still in our possession ? "

" Yes, Mr. Cowran, they are."

" Is Mr. Golding aware of that fact ? "

" As to that I can't say. He never has applied to us for them. I should have thought he would have done so, for they are the kind of things a man wouldn't wish to have out of his reach."

" Because they would reveal the secret of his business combinations—eh ? "

" That's what I mean, Mr. Cowran."

" Do you know where they are ? "

" The papers ? Yes, sir. They are in the same old deed box that was used before we ceased to act for Mr. Golding. It's the last on the left, second row from bottom."

" I want you to get them out to-morrow. I wish to look them over."

" Do you wish to have them returned to Mr. Golding, sir ? "

" Hum ! Well—yes—possibly. Meanwhile, I wish copies to be made of them."

" Hand or type-writer ? "

" Type-writer will do. Let's see—Miss Claver-house, isn't it ? "

" Miss Claverhouse—yes."

" She can be depended on, of course—doesn't gossip, and all that ? "

" I can guarantee her being perfectly discreet, Mr. Cowran."

" And I daresay you could guarantee her pos-

sessing all the other feminine virtues—eh, Talbot?
Well, that's all right.   Let her copy them to-morrow.   She can finish them in one day, can't she?"

"Easily, I should say, Mr. Cowran."

Here the dialogue ceased.   The clerk returned
to his references, and Cowran put on his hat and
coat and left the office, with a thoughtful air and a
gathering frown upon his brow.

CHAPTER VII.

TALBOT AND HIS FRIENDS.

JOHN TALBOT, the clerk of Conran and Co., lived in a little flat somewhere between Washington Square and Sixth Avenue. It was on the fifth floor, and there was nothing above it except some chambers for servants, the roof, and the sky. There was no elevator in the building, and the stairs by which the several flats communicated with the outside world were narrow and dark. But when you had mounted to John Talbot's door, and, leaving your hat and coat in the little dark hall, had entered the sitting-room, you began to find it very pleasant.

Talbot lived with his old mother, whose idol he was, and who cared for him with the same solicitude and tenderness as when he was an infant in her arms ; she seemed scarcely to understand that he had grown to be a man, and was taking his own part in the world. Her imagination, inspired by her memory, still saw him attired in pinafore and short skirts ; and when he took her on his knee to caress and make much of her, it seemed to her, by some magic maternal perversity, that it was she who held him in her lap. She was a very religious old lady, and every evening, before they went to

bed, she read a chapter from the Bible to her son,
as she had done thirty years before, and ever since.
She knew nothing of worldly wickedness, save in
the abstract theological sense ; and she could
hardly have been more shocked at a murder than
she was at a fib, or at the idea of drinking a glass
of toddy or smoking a cigar. Talbot was certainly
guilty, though in strict moderation, of both of the
latter crimes, and possibly they had led him into
the fibbing pitfall, when his mother brought up the
subject of those evil indulgences for discussion. But
if his garments ever smelt of tobacco, or his breath
of whisky, she did not know it ; not because she
could not smell, but because she did not know that
tobacco and whisky produced those aromas, but,
like the ancient Roman's wife, took it for granted
that all men smelt like that.

Talbot was a steady worker, and as regular as a
pendulum ; but he found time for other things besides looking up references and writing lawyers'
letters. His taste was for things in the way of art,
and he made it serviceable for the adornment of
his rooms. The walls were hung (by John's own
hand) with papers which were pleasing in hue and
design, and had the additional merit of not costing
much. He devoted a good deal of thought and ingenuity to the friezes and dados, and mitigated the
blankness of the ceilings by washes of a warm tone
that harmonized with the papers. From various
sources he had collected prints, etchings, and pho-
tographs, which he framed and hung up ; and he

spent the leisure hours of several weeks in constructing a set of bookshelves that filled the spaces not occupied by the doors and windows in one of the rooms. These shelves he then gradually stocked with books, giving much pains and thought to their selection, his aim being that they should be not only of good literary repute, but readable into the bargain. He got Milton, perhaps in deference to his mother ; Shakespeare he got for himself ; he owned a copy of "Tom Jones," but Johnson's "Rasselas" was not among his possessions. He bought a number of comfortable chairs, in which to sit while reading his volumes, and a broad-seated sofa for his mother to lie down upon when she felt tired. They did not keep a servant of their own, but the wife of the janitor, for a consideration, did the rough part of the work, leaving old Mrs. Talbot to cook her son's breakfast and dinner, and perform such dusting and polishing and setting-in-order as could be properly performed only by a mother or a wife. With the latter commodity and crown of domestic happiness, John Talbot, at thirty years of age, was unprovided. Perhaps this was the result of his own fastidiousness or lack of social opportunities ; perhaps a lack of appreciativeness on the ladies' part was to blame; or perhaps John felt that his mother would be a critic much less easily satisfied than himself. At all events, he was still a bachelor, though signs were not wanting that he had registered no vows of perpetual celibacy.

In fact—and it was a fact which, as we have
seen, had not escaped the eye of Gilbert Cowran—
Talbot was at this very time in the throes of an affair of the heart with no less a personage than Mr.
Cowran's type-writer,—the young lady, that is to
say, not the instrument. She had been in the office several months, and had acquitted herself ad-
mirably ; she hardly made a mistake once a day,
and she was always ready and good-humored. She
had short hair—the tendency of literary pursuits is
to lengthen the locks of the male practitioner, and
to curtail those of the female—a turned-up nose,
and spectacles ; but you could not talk with her
ten minutes without liking her, and feeling convinced of her indestructible goodness. Though
she never allowed any thing to interfere with her
official duties, she was an extremely sociable little
body, and loved talking better than reading, or
than any thing else, except, perhaps, John Talbot
himself, whose long, lank, and melancholy-looking
figure had captivated her maiden fancy from an
early period of their acquaintance ; possibly it was
a reflection of her tender cordiality which first apprised John that his own affections were breaking
loose. Though John's visage was cast in a melan-
choly mold, it was by no means the harbinger of
a morose disposition ; on the contrary, he was full
of a fine dry humor, which, like wine, he kept
for the use of his intimate friends. He looked like
an ascetic monk of the order of Flagellants ; but if
monasteries produced such fruit as he it would be

impossible to keep the gentler sex out of them. His face was that of a suffering Jesuit, but his heart was as warm and tender as a child's, and his imagination teemed with quaint and funny conceits, which never ran dry, and yet were never in excess of the demand. You had to learn how to take him (which you could do only if you yourself had certain human and enlightened qualities) and thereafter he was inexhaustibly good company. . The women who knew him thought of him as a brother, and to children he appeared like a father. But Miss Betty Claverhouse, the type-writer at Cowran's, was simply in love with him ; and that, of course, was different.

Talbot's friends were not numbered by hundreds, nor even by scores, for he was not a club man, or a frequenter of fashionable society ; but there were one or two fellows whom he liked, and who liked him, and one of these was a young gentleman by the name of Cunliffe. The attentive reader has already heard of Frank Cunliffe, but has not yet been regularly introduced to him. Cunliffe and Talbot were so different from each other, and lived in such alien regions, that it is necessary to account for their knowing each other.

Frank Cunliffe was the son of a rich man who lost nearly all he had soon after Frank got through college. This was awkward for the old gentleman, of course, and he did not long survive it ; but it was also awkward for the son, because he had been brought up in luxury, and with no expecta-

tion of being obliged to work for a living. To make
matters worse, he was not absolutely obliged to
work for a living, though his acquaintances all said
that he ought to do so. His father's estate, when
settled, yielded an income which just enabled him
to pay his dues at his club and his annual bill at
his tailor's.

When the dictionary of misfortunes which are
considered rather lucky by the victims of them
comes to be written, this particular species of mis-
fortune will occupy a prominent place in it. It en-
ables a man to command some of the luxuries of
life, but few or none of its comforts. He feels the
ability to work, and recognizes, in the abstract,
that work would better his condition, but he is re-
luctant to break with the traditions of gentility,
and to admit what he would call the tradesman's
spirit ; and besides, among the many things which
he knows he could do, it is difficult to decide which
would be best worth doing. Meanwhile there is the
club, and the social whirligig continually revolving,
and the human *vis inertiæ*—emphasized, very likely,
by a temperamental disposition to indolence—and
it is really no wonder that these poor fellows never
come to anything. Nor is their fate always merely
relative ; occasionally their little income gets
raided, or they fall into some snare or other, and
then they are forlorn indeed. They hang on by
hook or by crook, as long as they can ; and at last
disappear, and no one asks after them, for fear
of hearing something unpleasant.

· Frank Cunliffe had not got beyond the negative stage. Perhaps he was a trifle to windward even of that. He had had a dramatic instinct in him from a boy, and had several times seriously considered the question of going on the stage. He was sure that he would have made a great success of it; and possibly he might have trained himself into a tolerable actor. He had a good figure and presence ; he was handsome enough, and his voice was full and clear, and agreeably modulated for an American. He knew a great many actors, and several actresses, and was a regular first-nighter at all the theaters ; but, somehow, he never entered the profession, and he had the good sense not to indulge in amateur theatricals. One thing he did do. After some years, he wrote, more for a lark than in earnest, a criticism of a play that had just been produced, and sent it to a daily paper. The regular dramatic critic of this paper happened on that day to be suffering from an attack of *spiritus frumenti* and had not come to time with his copy ; the editor printed Cunliffe's, had an interview with him, and offered him a regular engagement. Cunliffe hemmed and hah'd, and finally accepted it on condition that his secret should be kept. So he wrote under an assumed name, and every body for whose sake he had assumed it knew the secret immediately ; the public read the criticisms, which were clever, and neither knew nor cared who " Faust, Jr.," was. Cunliffe's salary enabled him to smoke

twenty-dollar cigars, instead of fifteen-dollar ones,
as heretofore.

However, he became something of a power in the
New York theatrical world, and at length an opportunity occurred to put this power to some practical
use.   Cunliffe had a young relative—a second
cousin once removed, or something of that kind—
who possessed an unusually good contralto voice,
and had learned how to use it.   Though winning
to the ear, this young lady was not correspondingly
attractive to the eye.   She had light hair, a dull
complexion, gray eyes, and irregular features.
She was flat-chested and could not walk gracefully.
She was an orphan, poor, and ambitious.   She
wrote a letter to Cunliffe, and asked him to help
her to get an engagement to sing in concert.

Cunliffe had never seen her.   He called on her,
and at the first glimpse of her was completely dis-
couraged.   She chatted with him awhile, and he
discovered that she was entertaining and original.
She sat down at her piano and sang to him, and he
told her to put on her bonnet and come with him
to the impresario's.

The emotional gamut through which the impresario passed was a repetition of Cunliffe's experience.   When the girl had sung to him, he engaged
her at a higher salary than she or her cousin had
anticipated : and then he set himself to solve the
problem of making her (for public purposes) better
looking.

Her head was square and rather too large, but it

was full of solid sense, and instead of being
offended at the impresario's criticisms of her personal appearance, she received them cordially and
archly, and entered into his suggestions and per-
plexities with earnest and helpful sympathy. As
for her figure, that was an easy matter. Any thing
can be made of a figure, provided it is not too fat
to begin with—as this young lady's was not. "We
will assume that you are provided with a perfect
figure," said the impresario, "but now for your
face!" "Ah! that will tax your magic," remarked
the lady, with kindly compassion: "but at any
rate I can have a wig." "The hair will not be
impossible," the impresario replied: "and when
you have your new complexion, I do not despair of
your eyes—with eyebrows, of course. But your
nose and mouth—they are really—in fact they
are——" The lady laughed, showing a row of excellent teeth, and interrupted him: "They are
terrible, I know; but hear me sing again!" With
that she opened her irremediable mouth and sent
forth from it a flood of music so powerful, so cap-
tivating, and withal so afire with passion—a passion
that she had not betrayed in her previous efforts—
that both the impresario and Cunliffe were star-
tled and delighted. It was only a bar or two, and
then she stopped. "Did you see my nose then?"
"I forgot all about it." "Then perhaps the audience will too." And so it proved. Miss Kitty
Clive (such was the stage name which she chose to
assume, and under which she will figure in this his-

tory) became very popular with the public, who
never suspected that she was physically a fright.
And truly she did not look so, behind the foot-
lights, with the aids of art, music, and excitement.
She had a deep nature, too, and somehow that told.
Cunliffe was immensely proud of his protégée, as
he liked to call her. And she was grateful to
him, a rare thing in women, who are apt to hate
those from whom they have received practical
benefits.

Now when Miss Kitty Clive had sung for six
months under the impresario who first secured her
services, she received an offer from another manager, with a promise of double her then salary. She
accepted it, but was informed by her original pro-
prietor that she was bound to him, and that he
would not let her go. She told him that she would
consent to remain with him if he would pay her the
sum that was tendered by his rival ; he refused ;
and on her attempting to carry out her purpose, he
applied for and obtained an injunction restraining
her from singing in any establishment but his
own.

In this dilemma, she turned for assistance to her
cousin Frank : and he, upon learning the state of
affairs, applied to the best lawyer he knew of to
plead her case. This lawyer happened to be Gilbert Cowran, whom Cunliffe was already slightly
acquainted with from having met him at the club.
His visits to the office, during the progress of the
case (which was carried to a successful issue for

Miss Kitty Clive), were the means of making known
to him Mr. John Talbot, and various circumstances
served to cement their friendship. Their mutual
desire to see more of each other led Talbot, after
some hesitation, to ask Cunliffe to spend an evening at his house. Cunliffe came, and afterward
came again, bringing Kitty Clive with him. Talbot,
on his side, invited Miss Betty Claverhouse ; old
Mrs. Talbot acted as duenna for the party ; Kitty
sang, Betty chatted, and they had a lovely evening.
This event occurred on a Sunday, that being the
only day of the week on which Kitty had her liberty.
A few Sundays later, the meeting was repeated,
with even more agreeable results, and by degrees
it became a custom with these good young people
to assemble at Talbot's rooms on the coming of
each Sabbath. On these occasions they were a
close corporation ; no outsiders were admitted. It
would have been even nicer, perhaps, if Kitty and
Frank had been lovers, as well as John and Betty.
But although Frank was very fond of his cousin,
and proud of her talents, he was not the sort of
man to feel a passion for her, being a great wor-
shiper of physical beauty, for one thing, and
probably unable to appreciate at their true value
the really great qualities of soul that Kitty possessed. Besides, he had made up his mind long
before that marriage was not one of the luxuries in
which he could afford to indulge : for he would not
marry a poor woman, and he was too poor to
marry a rich one. Meanwhile John and Betty did

their best to be in love enough for all four, and succeeded very fairly.

About a month before our story opens, however, a serious catastrophe occurred to one of the number of the quartette, which threw a gloom over them all. Frank Cunliffe received a "pointer" direct from headquarters ; it was the opportunity of a lifetime ; an ample fortune was to be made for an outlay of twenty thousand dollars. Frank resisted, called all his worldly wisdom and experience to his aid, told himself that he was too old a bird to be caught with that chaff, overcame the temptation, went to bed, dreamed of a hundred thousand dollars, went down to a broker's in the morning, put up his margins, and in three days thereafter was left with but five thousand dollars in the world. That is the sort of man he was, and the sort of luck he had.

CHAPTER VIII.

CUNLIFF'S TROUBLES.

THAT night Cunliffe did not feel in spirits for the club, so he went to the theater and heard Kitty sing. She was in good voice, and looked astonishingly well. She recognized Frank in the audience, and sang to him. The music soothed and consoled him for the time being. After the performance he went round to the stage door, and when Kitty came out he offered her his arm, and they walked through the snow together to her lodgings.

On the way he told her what had happened.

Kitty listened to him without making any comment, but with a manner, and a closeness of attention which were in themselves better than most kinds of expressed sympathy and consolation. This was a way she had. After the story was told, she asked him whether the person who gave him the "pointer" had intended to deceive him.

"Not at all," was the reply. "He was all right. He lost himself, but he could afford it. We were both of us fooled, that's all."

"Who fooled you?"

"Nobody can tell that. It was a deal; some

one of the big men selling to and buying from himself—the old story in short. He may have had a far-reaching purpose in doing it, or he may have wanted to give the boys a whirl, as they call it. At all events, he has whirled me out of the world I have lived in, and into I don't know what—the income of five thousand dollars at six per cent. ! "

" Twenty thousand dollars, was it ? "

" Never mind ; the milk is spilt, and the fat is in the fire ; but such things happen every day. It serves me right, Kitty, for being a fool with my eyes open. Let's talk of something else. You were great this evening ! "

" I am making a great deal of money, Frank ; and I owe it all to you."

" To me ! Did I sing for you ? You are a good girl, and you will make your way. I only hope you won't go and marry some idiot ! "

Kitty laughed. " Blessed be my ugliness. I couldn't do it even if I wanted to."

" You're not ugly. I'd rather have you as you are than the handsomest girl in New York. Besides you look a hundred per cent. better than you did when you began. They talk against the stage ; but I believe that it is the best thing a good woman can get onto. She's independent, she's occupied, and she's in the midst of life."

" Why don't you try it, Frank ? You would do well and be happy."

" Oh, my dear, it's much too late to think of that. If I had begun when I was fourteen, or even

twenty-one, I might have had a show ; but I'm too
much set in my ways to be licked into shape now.
If I had a voice, like you, it would be different ;
but to be an actor—to identify myself with the
characters of imaginary people—my joints have
grown too stiff ! Besides, I have some vanity left,
God knows why ; and I couldn't stand having the
fellows at the club come round to criticise my
début. No, I can't get out of the hole by that
route."

A short silence followed this statement.

"It seems to me," said Kitty at last, "that the
men who do these things ought to be punished in
some way."

"What men do you mean, my dear ?"

"The men who get up these panics on the street,
and ruin people."

"Oh, if a fellow jumps into the lion's den, it's
his own fault if he gets scratched. He wasn't
obliged to go there. The very man who cleaned
me out has probably suffered himself in the same
way in the past, and now he is having his innings.
I suffer because I happen to be in the way. It's
give and take—the way of the world ! "

"But why should you suffer ? You had not injured this man, and he has no right to harm innocent people because somebody who was not innocent harmed him."

"That's abstract morality, but it's not human
nature. The way of Wall Street is the same principle they go on in college. Every Sophomore

class hazes the Freshmen. The Freshmen have
never done the Sophomores any harm; but the
Sophomores, when they were Freshmen, were
hazed by the class that were Sophomores then; and
they pay off their scores in that way."

"It is a senseless way; there is no justice in it.
If a man has been unfairly dealt with, and knows
by experience what it is, there is all the more reason why he should not deal unfairly with others.
If a man strikes you, I can understand that you
should strike him back; but I don't understand
why you should strike somebody else."

"I agree with your arguments," said Frank,
laughing, " and all I can say is that life is not
transacted in accordance with syllogisms. Meanwhile, you needn't be at all uneasy about me,
Kitty. I have five thousand dollars, and that will
last me five years, with proper economy. No one
but you knows I've been hit. In five years any
thing may happen—an uncle in California for instance! And now here we are at your house. I
wish it was Sunday; we could go 'round to Talbot's."

"I should like to do something," said Kitty,
giving him her hand.

"I want nothing better than to hear you sing
once in a while," he replied; and with that they
parted.

The next few weeks were busy ones for Frank
Cunliffe, who was obliged to devise some plan of
carrying on life for the future. His five thousand

dollars were invested in mortgages on real estate and brought ten per cent. interest ; but although many gentlemen can subsist on five hundred per annum, Cunliffe had never learned the art. His salary as dramatic critic amounted to about three hundred dollars. If he could, from any source, get an annual stipend of eight hundred or a thousand dollars more, he might scrape along. As to leaving New York, and burying himself in the country, he did not contemplate it ; it would be burial indeed. But, again, to live in New York meant to live in and with the club ; and the dues of that association would make a terrible hole in his income. The divisor was too big for the dividend. He turned the problem over and over and over in his mind, though he knew beforehand that a solution was impossible. He began to feel despondent, and the chance word that Kitty let fall—that the man who had done him this injury ought to be punished—recurred to his memory. He knew, or thought he knew, who that man was. But how could he be punished ? After all, it would be just as well if he could be induced to refund the twenty thousand dollars. Suppose Cunliffe were to walk into the great financier's office, state his case, and request him to write a check for the amount ? Why not ? What was twenty thousand dollars to a man like Golding ? Why should he not hand over the check and dismiss the applicant with his blessing, and an injunction to let this be a warning to him never to meddle with

Wall Street again? Cunliffe laughed aloud at the grotesque flights of his own imagination.

Some time passed, therefore, before he again felt in the mood to meet the little Sunday circle at Talbot's. But at length he sent a note to Kitty, to say that he would call for her that evening, and he found her waiting for him when he arrived. They had not met since their conversation about his calamity.

" Sit down a moment while I put on my bonnet," she said, throwing aside a copy of a newspaper which she had been reading, and greeting him with a warm clasp of the hand. " Let me look at you— are you sad or merry? You are thinner and paler; you have been troubled. My poor boy ! "

" Oh, I haven't begun to starve yet," returned Cunliffe, in the ironic tone that he had fallen into the habit of using, when referring to himself. " My friends continue to invite me to dinner, because they don't know that I am four-fifths poorer than I used to be."

" Are your club dues paid? "

" They won't be called for until next January, and then I can pretend forgetfulness for a month or two. By that time I may get a chance to rob or murder some one and devote the proceeds to the charitable purpose of paying them."

" Do you know, Frank," she said, looking thoughtfully at him, " I have a presentiment that there is going to be a change in your luck—that something will happen to put you back where you were before ? You were joking about an uncle in California the other day ; why might not something of the sort come true ? You have done nothing to deserve this trouble ? "

" If my uncle in California is going to leave me a fortune before next quarter day, it is high time that he was born ; I have yet to learn, at least, that that auspicious event has occurred. Come, my dear, don't let us talk nonsense. I have had presentiments, too ; and perhaps I have been tempted to turn them into realities. Time will show ; meanwhile, go and put on your bonnet, like a good girl. The Talbots will be expecting us. I wonder what these good people would say if they knew they were entertaining a pauper. Would they kick me out ?

Kitty sighed. " I don't blame you for being cynical, Frank," she said ; " but you needn't mistrust John Talbot. He is a good fellow. You have friends, you know. You will always have— friends who would do any thing for you."

She disappeared into her dressing-room, and Cunliffe took up the newspaper and ran his eye over it till she returned, dressed for the street. By that time he had regained his equanimity and good humor. Being no longer thus preoccupied, he fancied he perceived a subdued excitement in Kitty's manner that he had not had leisure to notice before. Her gray eyes looked dark and bright.

" How well that bonnet becomes you, Kitty," he said. " What a fine girl you are, anyhow ! I declare, I'm proud to be on the street with you. Some fellow will be coming in and stealing you away from me before long !"

" Is that prophecy accidental or premeditated ?" she asked, with a peculiar smile.

" What do you mean ? "

" Well, I was just going to tell you something, and it came in so aptly. The fact is—I really have got an admirer at last !"

" You speak as if you expected me to be surprised. Don't I tell you that I've been expecting it ever since you went on ? Who is he ? I want to kill him ! "

" Kill him for thinking me nice ? That's severe on him—and me ! "

" You know what I mean. The impertinent young whipper-snapper ! I hope you boxed his ears, at least ! "

" He isn't the kind of man to be boxed on the ear," she rejoined, laughing. " Nobody would ever think of such a thing."

" Oh, he is fascinating, is he ? Worse and worse ! "

" He is a very agreeable and intellectual gentleman."

" The deuce ! Is he anyone I know ? "

" I think not. He has been an officer of the regular army—General Stuart Weymouth."

" A general in the regular army ! He can be no chicken, then ! "

" No, not exactly. He is about fifty-five, I suppose."

" Oh ! Is he wealthy ? "

" I haven't asked him ; but I imagine he is not.
He was wounded in the war, and is living on half-
pay, or a pension, or whatever it is they give them."

" A battle-scarred veteran, eh ? Is he fine-looking ? "

" He is tall and soldierly-looking, with dark eyes
and a gray mustache. He is rather eccentric ; he
is entirely alone in the world, he says, and knows
very few people. He lives in a couple of rooms in
a lodging-house on Irving Place. But years ago
he used to be quite a prominent personage. He has
met all the distinguished people of the day. He
used to be acquainted with Mr. Golding, and Mr.
Golding offered him fifty thousand a year to let his
name be used as president of a company. But I
will tell you the rest some other time. Here we
are at the Talbots' ! "

CHAPTER IX.

A CUP OF TEA.

MISS BETTY CLAVERHOUSE had already arrived, and was chatting in her customary animated style with old Mrs. Talbot, while John sat by giving the finishing touches to a carved wooden bracket that he had been making. Mrs. Talbot was not altogether convinced whether it was right for John to do any thing of that kind on Sunday. But John had explained to her that he was not paid for doing it ; that, so far as it was ornamental, it was of no use, and that therefore, though he worked upon it, it was not working in the sense intended by the Mosaic law. " It isn't I that am to blame, mother," he added, " it's the dictionary, which makes me say I am ' working ' when in fact I am only improving my mind and æsthetic taste. You would not have me keep my hands idle, would you ? You know what Dr. Watts says ! "

" I sometimes think you are not in earnest, John," the old lady said, looking at him through her spectacles with a fond but doubtful expression.

" Ask Betty ; she knows," he replied. " I told her the other day that I thought she was a nice girl, and she believed I was in earnest then and there—didn't you, Bet?"

Bettie uplifted her nose and laughed.

"And yet that was on a Sunday; and it was much harder work than this," he rejoined, holding the bracket up to the light and regarding it with critical approval. "You would never believe, mother, what hard work it is to make Betty believe she is nice!"

"I shall never be as nice as I ought to be—since you think I'm nice," said Betty, finishing her laugh with a sigh.

"There! see what I told you! Well, very likely I am the victim of a delusion, and Bettie is a selfish, designing, ill-tempered hussy! What does an innocent boy like me know about women? Betty, did you finish that copying you had to do to-day?"

"Yes, John, every word of it. What is Mr. Cowran going to do with it?"

"Keep it, I suppose, as a souvenir of you. By the way, I have long felt uneasy about that man's attitude toward you. I suspect him of being my rival. But let him beware! I am appalling when my jealousy is aroused. If he ever ventures to betray his passion in any other way than by raising your salary, I shall give him a month's warning."

"Oh, I dare say! And where would your bread and butter come from?"

"Ha! You have no conception, girl, of the depth and subtlety of my schemes," said John, in his deepest bass voice. "I should take that copy of

Mr. Golding's private papers that you have just finished making, put them in my pocket, and pay Mr. Golding a call. I should tell him that unless he admitted me into full partnership with him on the spot, those secret memoranda should be published in every newspaper in this continent. Poor man ! Methinks I see him cower and accede ! "

At this juncture the door-bell rang ; and John, putting down his bracket, and leaving the two women to digest his pronunciamento as best they might, stalked with his long legs into the hall, and presently reappeared conducting Kitty Clive and Frank Cunliffe, fresh from their walk. There were cordial greetings all round, and then the little party drew their chairs round the fire-place, and prepared to enjoy themselves.

" What have you two been doing with yourselves this month past ? " Talbot asked. " Not marrying each other, I hope ! "

" And why not, pray ? " Cunliffe demanded.

" Well, for one thing, Betty and I want you and Miss Clive to be our best man and bridesmaid, respectively, and your marriage would balk our design. Besides, we shall wish to have some young unmarried people about us, to learn from our example how an ideal marriage should be carried on."

"You have found your ideal, then ? " said Kitty.

" There is one wrinkle in the rose-leaf—the future Mrs. Talbot's nose. I have a misgiving that snub-noses are not ideal. But I have consulted an eminent surgeon on the subject, and he informs me that by making an incision down the lady's nose, removing a part of the tissue, and inserting a silver cartilage, it can be transformed into an Arabian aquiline. It is a great comfort to think of it."

" Why, John, I am sure, when it came to the point, you would not be so barbarous ! " remonstrated his mother. "And I think people should be content with the features the Lord gave them—He knows best."

"You forget, mother, that Betty's feature (to call it that) was brought to its present altitude, not by the Creator's fiat, but by holding it against the grindstone. Her circumstances, heretofore, have been arduous and lowly. But now that she is about to be uplifted, as my wife, to aristocratic regions, it is right and proper that her nose should cease to be a reminder of her humbler state."

" Let my nose alone ! " exclaimed Betty indignantly. " I'm sure it's a great deal more likely to be held to the grindstone after our marriage than before ! "

" Have I not told you that I am about to become Mr. Golding's partner ! " returned John, with a superb gesture. " Do you imagine that there are any grindstones—or snub noses—about his premises ? "

" Mr. Golding's partner ! What are you talking about ? " cried Cunliffe.

"It's only some more of his nonsense," said Betty. "I was given some of Mr. Golding's secret papers to copy at the office, and ——"

"Betty, before you monopolize all the conversation, let me remind you that the tea is still in the caddy," Talbot interposed. "I like my wives to be not only aquiline, but active in the performance of domestic amenities. Run and see if the kettle boils."

"I will help you, Betty," said Kitty Clive, rising. "I know a new way of making tea—a secret of the mandarins'—and since you are to be married, I'll teach it to you." So the two young women went out together.

"I wasn't aware that Cowran did business for Golding now," Cunliffe remarked. "Has that quarrel of theirs been made up?"

"No, and I guess it won't be," Talbot replied. "This is an old affair—dating back to before the epoch of the quarrel, in fact."

"I see! Golding had deposited some of his private records with Cowran, and forgot all about it. But will Cowran use them against him?"

"I should rather suppose that he meant to return them, and has had the copies made for his own personal satisfaction or protection. It's not my business to make any suppositions on the subject, though. But I like the idea of Cowran's sending them back. It's as much as to say, 'I might get even with you if I chose, but I won't condescend to it.'"

" The papers are compromising, then ? "

" Not in a criminal sense, of course ; but Golding would wish to retain them for the same reason that a general in a campaign wishes to keep his strategic memoranda out of the enemy's hands. They would give him away."

" What sort of a fellow do you take Golding to be ?"

" Oh, well, he's a sort of ogre ; but I admire him. He is alive ; and he has communicated his life to every dollar of his two hundred millions. There is no rubbish in his workshop. He conducts his operations very much as a mathematician performs his calculations ; the experiment—the abstraction— is all he cares for. He might starve a whole town to death for the sake of carrying out a combination, but in spite of that I believe that the broad issue of his doings is beneficial to civilization. You can't estimate him as you would other men ; he is a genius ; he is like nature ; he has his destructive winters, but by and by you find that they are followed by spring and summer and autumn. It is impossible for a really great man not to do more good than evil."

" He may be a genius ; but he is the evil genius of a great many poor devils," observed Cunliffe. " I must say, if I were Cowran I should feel disposed to ' condescend ' a little !"

" You are one of those fellows who are always imagining that they would be worse than they are if they were some other fellow," returned Talbot,

passing his hand down over his long pale face and
yawning audibly. "I shall be asleep if those
girls don't bring that mandarin tea pretty quick.
Hi! Betty!"

"Here we come," replied Betty, entering with
the teapot and cups, and followed by Kitty with a
tray of toast and cake. "Oh, this tea is good! I
believe Kitty to be a Chinese in disguise!"

"I have heard that there is a handsome mandarin
watching about the stage-door of the theater," said
Talbot.

"You have been misinformed," interposed Cunliffe; "it is an American general, and his name is
Stuart Weymouth. He's a tall, fine-looking,
middle-aged gentleman, with a gray mustache and
dark eyes. He has been solitary and eccentric for
years, but Kitty's voice has lured him from retirement. He once refused an offer of fifty thousand
a year from Golding for the use of his name to
float a company. That's as far as I've heard yet.
Kitty, tell us the rest! How did he get introduced
to you?"

"There was nothing particularly romantic
about that part of it," Kitty replied. "He made
himself known to the manager, and asked him to
present him. The manager asked my permission,
and I gave it. I received General Weymouth in
the green-room. He told me that he came to the
theater accidentally six weeks before. Music was
the only enjoyment he had left in the world, and he
was in the habit of attending the operas and con-

certs at at the Academy of Music and Metropolitan ; but it was unusual for him to go to any of the
minor places. However, he said that after hearing
me on that first occasion he had not missed a
single performance since. He said there was a
quality in my voice that attracted him more than
any other voice he had heard. At first he had no
intention of making my personal acquaintance ;
but he had finally come to the conclusion that there
must be something in me that corresponded to my
voice, and that if he neglected to get an introduction
to me he would regret it the rest of his life, and he
was kind enough to add that he was now assured
that his intuition had not misled him, and begged
I would regard him thenceforth as a sincere admirer and faithful friend.''

" Sir Charles Grandison !" said Talbot.

" But that isn't all," exclaimed Frank Cunliffe.
" He offered to make you Mrs. General Weymouth, didn't he ? "

" If he did," replied Kitty, quietly, " I don't
see why I should speak about it. He is a gentleman, and I am not going to make game of
him."

" I remember him now," said Talbot. " I have
heard Golding speak of him. He had a good deal
of influence, social and political, at one time. But
something seemed to happen to him, and he disappeared. I guess he was generally believed to
be dead. I don't suppose his name would bring
fifty thousand a year now."

" Perhaps he had a ' pull ' on Golding," Cun-liffe suggested.

" I don't know any thing about that," said Talbot.

" If you mean that the fifty thousand dollars was a bribe to him to keep quiet about something injurious to Mr. Golding, his not accepting it would mean that he did not intend to keep quiet. But he has revealed nothing ; so it is unlikely that he had any thing to reveal." This was from Kitty.

" Did he talk much to you about Golding ? " Cunliffe asked.

" Not very much. He spoke of him in a friendly way. He said something about renewing their acquaintance."

" There is a mystery about him ! " Cunliffe declared.

" I don't like mysterious people, do you ? " said Miss Betty Claverhouse. " I like people one knows all about, like—like John ! "

" Think you to fathom me, slight girl ? " retorted her lover. " I am an abyss ! Hasten to fill me with another stoup of tea ! " This restored the easy tone of the conversation, but it thenceforth contained nothing important to this history.

CHAPTER X.

A SLEIGH-RIDE.

ANOTHER fall of snow, coming at this time, made capital sleighing in Central Park, and fashionable New York hastened to take advantage of it. The air was cold, but there was no wind, except such as was created by the swift movement of the sleighs. The sun was out in a cloudless sky, and there was sparkle and exhilaration everywhere. The soft jingling of the bells, now near, now far, but always audible, sounded a fitting accompaniment to the dancing of the blood in youthful veins. Those graceful cutters, that were gone before you could utter your admiration, contained many happy pairs of lovers, who, bundled up in soft furs and buffalo robes, imagined that life would glide along as smoothly as the sleigh—at least, as swiftly ! The horses seemed to enjoy the fun as much as the lovers ; they laid back their ears, and settled low down on their flying legs, and the white track slipped away beneath them like the surface of a cataract. It was glorious sport. On the lake the snow had been swept away, and the skaters were circling and wavering in inextricable convolutions. The boughs of the trees, so long bare of foliage, were now weighted with soft

burdens of snow, which the still air had suffered to
remain as it had fallen.　Kemeys's bronze panther,
crouching for her spring on the rock that overhangs
the drive, seemed to have just thrust her terrible
head out of the white blanket in which she had
been biding her time.　Cleopatra's Needle stood
slim and erect on its bleak mound, like a soldier
frozen at his post in a strange land, after standing
guard for twenty centuries on the banks of the
mysterious river, beneath the scorching suns of
Egypt.

One of the speediest of the cutters was occupied
by two gentlemen, who were so muffled up in fur
caps and collars that it was impossible to distinguish their features ; and they, on their side, made
no attempt to recognize any among the flying
crowd of sleighers.　The larger man of the two held
the reins, and kept his eyes on his horse's ears ;
but this occupation did not prevent him from
listening to what the other was saying, and occasionally interposing some remark or question of his
own.　No more secure place for a private and confidential dialogue could have been found than the
one they had chosen ; with all fashionable New
York around them, they were as unknown and as
unheard as if they had been on the lonely summit
of Mount Shasta or in the midst of the barren
deserts of Arizona.

"Your report of his conversation," said the
holder of the reins, "though it certainly doesn't
conflict with the theory of his guilt, does very little

towards clinching the proof of it. Golding has injured him, and he hates Golding for it. We knew as much before ; and there are probably a hundred men in New York to-day of whom the same is true. It is more to the purpose that some of his expressions indicated a willingness to contemplate violent measures. As for his conduct when you confronted him with the ' personal' in the paper, it is worth taking into consideration, and that is as much as can be said of it. It was a good point, and I am sorry it didn't effect a more definite result, one way or the other."

"It is also to be considered that no other man has appeared whom there is nearly as much reason to suspect as Cowran," remarked the other occupant of the sleigh. "Nothing in his record or situation is inconsistent with the theory. Ought not these facts to carry some weight?"

"They are merely negative. On the other hand, we have Cowran's character and temper. He has the name of being a bold man, one who fulfills his engagements, and has never been known to do any underhand work. His temper is warm, and when provoked he is inclined to violence. All that doesn't describe the sort of fellow who would write a series of anonymous letters."

"But the letters are violent enough, surely ! "

"In their expressions, but not in what we believe to be their intention—which is an important difference. They threaten Golding with death, but they do so only with the design of extorting money.

The letter which was received in answer to the second 'personal' removes all doubt on that point. Have you seen it?"

"No; I have only heard of it."

"It took up our suggestion as to a provision for his wife and family; and after a lot of palaver, and saying that he had no personal hostility against Golding, and would be willing to spare him if the Lord permitted, and so forth, the writer admitted that, although nothing would induce him to accept money for himself, still he might be induced to permit Mr. Golding to do something for those dependent upon him."

"And did he suggest any method of doing it?"

"Yes; and quite an ingenious one for a religious maniac. Mr. Golding is to give him advance information of the rise or fall of his stocks. This is to be done by advertisements in the "personal" column of one of the morning papers, the information being given in cipher."

"Is the cipher given too?"

"It is, and it is just the thing for the purpose: easily understood if you have the key, and not so peculiar as to excite curiosity in those not concerned. The whole thing was evidently planned out from the beginning. Finally he says that in case Golding gives any information which is not correct he may expect very short shrift; and he is left to infer that so long as the information brings money the Lord's vengeance will be delayed. The fellow is a contemptible hound, and that is why I find it difficult to reconcile him with what we know of Cowran. I could understand his killing a man in a fit of passion ; but this is a horse of quite another color."

" Will Mr. Golding give the information ? " inquired the other, after a pause.

" To be sure he will, and the fellow will make money on it. That seems to be about our only chance of identifying him."

" You mean that we can trace him by means of the brokers through whom he acts ? "

" But if he is as shrewd as he has proved himself to be thus far, he can elude us there without much difficulty. I was in hopes that he would have asked for a certain fixed sum of money ; I would have been sure of him then ! "

" But he won't be satisfied with one haul, do you think ? He'll be coming again and again, and sooner or later we must catch him napping."

" That's all very well ; but it would be more satisfactory to get at him more directly. You have visited Cowran's office, of course ? "

" I dropped in yesterday, on the pretext of getting him to lunch with me. There was nobody worth looking after there. A head-clerk named Talbot, a young woman to do the type-writing, and a couple of younger men. My impression was very strong that they are none of them in it. Cunliffe tells me that he has known Talbot for several years, and that he is as guileless as a baby."

" Is that Frank Cunliffe—a member of the League Club ? "

" That is the fellow."

" I had a glimpse of him the other evening. What do you know about him ? "

" He lives on his income, and ekes it out by doing dramatic criticism. He's a well-educated man, in the fashion, knows every body. Got acquainted with Cowran through some legal affair. But I haven't followed him up much."

" In an affair of this kind, when we are all in the dark, you should follow up every body. There's no telling where a clew might come in. Does this Cunliffe know Golding ? "

" I never heard him mention him."

" Find that out at once. How long has Talbot been in Cowran's office ? "

" Ten years at least."

" Then Talbot must know Golding, and all about his quarrel with Cowran ; and since Cunliffe knows Talbot, he is likely to at least have some useful knowledge about Golding. Why, there may be something in this ! The more I think about this business, the more inclined I am to believe that the man we want has no personal quarrel with Golding, but is simply a rascally speculator. If Cunliffe writes for the papers, his income can't be sufficient for him. The glimpse I had of his face didn't impress me favorably. Fellows like him, keeping up appearances in good society, are sometimes the most worthless kind of rogues. I would sooner

act upon slight evidence against a man like Cunliffe than upon strong evidence against a man like
Cowran."

"I will take him up immediately. Shall I keep
an eye on Talbot also?"

"Not for the present. We shall probably not
want him unless the scent after Cowran gets hotter
than it is ; and meanwhile you can keep track of him
sufficiently through Cunliffe. As you are practically
alone in the investigation of this affair—and, by
the way, what you have done has been well done,
all things considered—you had better not try to be
in too many places at once. Luckily, Cunliffe and
Cowran are both members of the same club, and
— Hullo !"

As he uttered the exclamation, he pulled in his
horse, and brought the sleigh to a standstill at the
side of the road. At the same time he pushed back
his fur cap from his forehead, and opened his fur
collar, revealing the well-known features of Inspector Byrnes. Another sleigh, advancing in the opposite direction, drew up abreast of him. It was
driven by a Cossack coachman, and contained Mr.
Owens.

"Excuse me for stopping you, Owens," said the
Inspector. "This is Mr. Hamilton, a friend of
mine, and on the case. I didn't wish to lose the
opportunity of asking you whether there was any
thing new."

"I'm glad we met," Owens replied. "There is

something new, and I confess it puzzles me. Two things, in fact."

" When can I see you ? "

" The best plan will be for us both to drive to my house. Mr. Hamilton will come too, of course. Will that suit you ? "

" Perfectly ! "

Mr. Owens spoke to his coachman, who turned the sleigh and set out homeward, followed by the Inspector and Hamilton.   In a short time the three men were seated at the table in Mr. Owens's library.

" You said there were two new things, I think," said the Inspector.

" I did, and I will give them to you in the order of their appearing.   The first is this letter from the unknown letter-writer.   Read it, and see what you think of it."

The Inspector took the letter, and perused it twice carefully.

" He replies to the advertisement," he then said, looking up, " and announces that he will follow Mr. Golding's advice on Wednesday as to buying stock."

" Yes ; and there is something else."

" So I see ; but I don't understand it.   It seems to refer to some previous business of Mr. Golding's of which I know nothing."

" I'll explain it to you.   At the time Golding quarreled with Cowran, Cowran had some papers of Golding's in his possession, to be used in conducting a certain law-suit. These papers were of a very private nature ; they contained the key to some of Golding's secret methods of conducting operations."

" I follow you. Go on."

" The contents of these papers were known to no one except Golding, Cowran, and myself. By some oversight, they have remained in Cowran's hands ever since. Golding thought they had been returned to him, but they had not."

" I understand ! And the expressions in this letter——"

" The expressions in that letter could have been used only by a man who was familiar with the contents of those papers."

" Humph ! " ejaculated Hamilton, glancing at his superior. " That seems to come pretty straight, doesn't it ? "

The Inspector stroked his chin and was silent for a few moments.

" Could Cowran have communicated the contents of the papers to any third party, during the interval between the quarrel and now ? " he demanded at length.

" It is physically possible, no doubt, but extremely improbable. He could have done so only with the intention of injuring Golding ; and the injury would have been infinitely more effective if, instead of telling the secret to one man, he had put it in the papers and published it to all the world."

" True.   Then you infer that Cowran wrote the letters ? "

" That would be the logical deduction ; nevertheless, I must confess that I still believe Cowran to be innocent.   Though he would not be likely to voluntarily betray the secret to any one, accident might have somehow revealed it without his connivance or knowledge.   But that is not all."

" Ah, to be sure ! You spoke of something else. What is it ? "

" Mr. Golding this morning received by a special messenger from Cowran's office, a sealed packet; he opened it and found—what do you suppose ? "

" The private papers ? "

" The private papers, complete and intact ! Now, Inspector, what is your interpretation of that ? "

" Were they accompanied by any letter or memorandum from Cowran ? "

" The messenger presented a receipt for Golding to sign.   That was all."

" Well," said the Inspector, after a pause, " that will bear thinking over ! It doesn't seem to hang together, and yet it's difficult to separate it.   What do you make out of it, Hamilton ? "

" It might be just a blind," Hamilton said.

" So it may," returned the Inspector, " and, on the other hand, I'd hardly venture to call it a coincidence.   Give me two days, Owens," he added, turning to that gentleman, " and I will at least tell you whether it's Cowran or, not.   Meanwhile— good-by ! "

CHAPTER XI.

GENERAL WEYMOUTH'S lodgings in Irving Place were neither spacious nor luxurious ; but they were characterized by soldierly neatness and order. There were two rooms, one facing on the street, and the other, communicating with it by a small bath-room, on the yard at the back of the house. The walls of the former room were decorated by a steel-engraved portrait of General Grant and another of Abraham Lincoln. There was a plain mahogany bookstand in one corner, containing almost nothing but poetry aud theology, these being, apparently, the only kinds of literature that the general cared for. In another corner was a violoncello—a fine instrument, though the general had insured the silent or open hostility of every one of his fellow-lodgers by his affection for and practice with it ; he was an early riser, and before breakfast was his chosen season for extracting what he was pleased to consider harmony from the strings of his overgrown fiddle. The general's habits were regular. For an hour after breakfast he read theology ; then he walked out, rain or shine, for an hour or two more. Toilet operations occupied him an hour more, and then he went down to the midday meal. In the afternoon he wrote letters, if he had any to write, or read poetry ; half an hour before dinner he took another short stroll. After dinner he went to the concert or the opera ; and before he went to bed, he took another dose of theology. He slept soundly in a narrow military cot, such as is used in camps ; he snored faithfully all night long ; and when he awoke in the morning the first object his eyes rested upon was a lithograph of Beethoven, which hung over the foot of the bed.

This was the daily routine of a man who had fought with honor and distinction in the civil war, and had for some years afterward occupied a prominent position in social and political life. His retirement from the world, whether voluntary or not, was at all events endured with dignity, and even with a kind of grave cheerfulness ; he made no complaints, nor was he addicted to buttonholing people with tales of his former importance and present unappreciated deserts. He simply held his tongue, was courteous and considerate (except in the matter of the violoncello), and minded nobody's business but his own.

Of late, however, those who were familiar with his ways had remarked a change in him. He frequently omitted his morning walk ; nor was his early matutinal practice with the 'cello as systematic and relentless as of yore. His step would be heard pacing backwards and forwards in his room for hours at a time ; and at table he was silent and preoccupied beyond his wont. His landlady became anxious, and ventured to ask him whether any thing was the matter, to which he replied that he was in perfect health. As he paid his rent in full on the ensuing quarter-day, she came to the conclusion that his troubles, if he had any, were no affair of hers, and forbore to question him further. He still went out every evening, but it was noticed that he came home rather later than usual.

One forenoon he informed her that he should not be home to lunch, as he had business down-town. He was absent accordingly, but returned late in the afternoon with a very gloomy brow, and he did not emerge again that day. The day following he appeared attired in his best clothes, and walked up the street with a measured and resolute step. Half an hour later he was admitted to the reception-room of the popular singer, Miss Kitty Clive.

Miss Clive soon came in, looking wholesome and cordial. Her professional career had certainly improved her appearance. She carried herself better ; her figure was fuller ; the imperfections of her complexion had disappeared. Then her expression was intelligent and sympathetic, and you felt there were reserves behind that could be made available upon occasion ; her smile was kind and her laugh merry. As for her voice, it was a revelation not only of melody, but of a deep and rich nature,

"It was good of you to come to me to-day, General Weymouth," she said, after the first greetings. "I have been feeling out of sorts all the morning. You always make me feel better contented with myself and things in general."

"I can understand," the general replied, "that the pleasure you give me must be something of a pleasure to yourself. That belongs to a generous and humane character like yours. But I design to try your good nature further than usual to-day. I wish to tell you something about myself."

"Then what you say can not fail to be interesting. But let me tell you first that I require no personal explanation at your hands. I value your friendship, and I respect you without need of any further warrant for it than is given by what I see and know of you. A woman depends more on her intuitions than on any formal recommendations, and my intuitions tell me that you are to be trusted."

"I thank you, my child, with all my heart," said the general. "Well, your trust is so far justified that I can say that my past life has been free from dishonorable reproach ; I have behaved as a soldier and a gentleman is bound to behave. But it was not a vindication that I was about to attempt. What I wish to say is prompted by the fact that it has a bearing upon my—our mutual attitude. It is necessary that you should know it in order to be able to judge intelligently of a matter which I intend afterwards to submit to you."

"You make me curious in spite of myself. Do let me hear!"

"I have already spoken to you about my former relations with the great financier, Maxwell Golding," the general began. "I mentioned that there had been a suggestion that I should be connected, on terms very favorable to myself, with the management of a large enterprise. I told you that I had declined the position. But I did not tell you why I had done so, nor why, after that event, my way of life became so different from what it had been before."

He paused, and bent his eyes upon the fire, pulling somewhat nervously at his gray mustache. Kitty regarded him thoughtfully, and sighed. He had been a handsome and gallant youth thirty years ago ; but time and trouble had had their inevitable effect upon him, as upon all men and women. Yet he had always remained a gentleman and a soldier. Must honor and sincerity forever be the passports to unhappiness? and if so, might there not be some justification for defying these traditions, and doing, upon occasion, what seems right in one's own eyes? If evil did not bear the stigma, would it be evil still?

"When I came out of the war," said the general, "I was thirty years old, and I had a considerable fortune. I had received a bullet through the upper part of the body, but the wound had healed, and I felt as if I had the better part of my life still before me. My family is of good origin and repute, and all doors were open to me. There seemed to be a likelihood of permanent peace ; I saw that my professional rank would be a sine-cure, or at least an idle routine; I did not wish to burden the government with my salary ; and so I resigned my commission.   I was interested in the reconstruction problem, and thus I came to take an active part in politics ; and the ambition grew upon me to introduce a better class of citizens to the control of affairs than had hitherto taken part in them, to make our politics worthy of our na-tional name and destiny.   It was a great scheme, and it had already suggested itself to many good men, as it will doubtless continue to do hereafter. Whether any practical good results will ever come from it, I will not pretend to say.   I can not con-gratulate myself upon my own success in the enter-prise.

"This activity of mine continued for several years.   I did not aim at holding offices myself ; my energies were directed to bringing honest and efficient men before the voters, and to making the voters realize the necessity of electing honest and efficient men.   Our national vice is an easy-going, cynical indifference ; we put up with abuses until they became despotisms ; and though we are apt to throw off the despotisms when they become too open and outrageous, yet the day may come when we shall encounter some despot who will not be de-posed.   It was not long before I came to the con-viction that the most dangerous despotism we

would have to deal with would be that of wealth.
Our country offers facilities for the amassing of
enormous fortunes in a comparatively short time ;
and there is no guarding against the contingency
of this wealth falling into ignorant or unprincipled
hands. Every body is in pursuit of money ; and
the man who gets the most will generally be considered the ablest man.

" I was approaching forty years of age when I
met the woman who afterwards became my wife.
Yes, Miss Clive, I have been married, though very
few people are aware of it. She was a beautiful
girl then—strikingly so ; and she was accomplished ; I took it for granted that she was every
thing else that was lovely in womanhood. As to
her origin, I did not inquire closely into it ; it is
not the custom in this country to worship ances-
tors. I was satisfied in believing that she loved
me and that she was lovable. We were engaged ;
and after a few months a clergyman pronounced
the marriage service over us.

" Our honeymoon lasted four weeks. The day after we returned, as I was sitting in my office down-
town, a card was brought in to me, and I was told
that the person whose name it bore was desirous of
seeing me. I gave orders that he be admitted. He
came in—a man of eight and twenty, handsome,
but with an air about him that I did not like—a
rascally air. His manner was polished, however ;
he was well-dressed, and seemed to be well-educated. I asked him what he wanted.

" He said, ' I must begin by telling you that the name on that card is not my real name. It is one I have assumed, for good and sufficient reasons. But I do not wish to approach you under false colors.'

"'I answered that I did not perceive how that concerned me.

" He said, ' It does concern you, though, more than any one else. I shall tell you my real name; but it will depend upon you whether any one else ever hears it.'

"'How does it concern me?' I asked. ' I never saw you before.'

"'Well,' he said. 'You know a man does not change his name for nothing. He has some reason for it. Either the name is an ugly or common one, and does not please his ear; or else he has done something to bring it into bad odor, and changes it to escape the consequences. The latter is my case!'

"'I ask you again,' I said, ' how does that concern me? If you are a rascal, as your words seem to imply, it is my concern to see that you leave this office, and don't return to it; but I have nothing further to do with you.'

" 'Yes, you have,' he said. ' And you will not turn me out of this office.'

" I began to think the man was crazy, or that he had mistaken me for somebody else. If I had been guilty of any rascality in the past, I should have supposed that he had become aware of it, and meant to make me pay for his knowledge. But my con-science was clear, and I had no fear of him or of any man. I decided to let him speak. 'Say what you have to say,' I told him, 'and then go.'

" ' Are we where no one can hear us ?' he asked. ' I make the inquiry in your interest quite as much as in mine.'

" I told him that he need be under no apprehen-sion of eavesdroppers.

" 'Then here it is,' said he. ' I was arrested three years ago for a certain crime. I needn't tell you what the crime was, for my real name will probably be sufficient to recall the crime to your memory.' Here he told me his real name ; and I did recognize it as that of the perpetrator of a dastardly roguery that had created a sensation at the time. ' I was tried and convicted,' he went on; ' and I may tell you in confidence that the jury were quite right ; I was guilty. The judge very properly sentenced me to fifteen years imprison-ment with hard labor. It was not too severe a sentence.'

" ' And this was only three years ago ?' I said.

" 'Only three years ago,' he answered ; ' and here I am again, as right as a trivet !'

" 'Have you broken jail ?'

" 'No ; and I haven't been pardoned out, either. I am out on better grounds than either of those. My lawyers discovered a flaw in the trial, and got me out on the technicality. I am just as free and as safe as if I had lived virtuous all my days.'

"'For the last time,' I said, 'what do you want?'

"'Well,' he said, 'ten thousand dollars will be enough for to-day; but I warn you that I shall need some more at the end of the month.'

"'You are welcome to ten thousand dollars,' I said, 'if you can get it. But meanwhile, get out of this room.'

"'If I leave this room,' he said, 'it will be to call on the lady who calls herself Mrs. Weymouth. I am confident that she will refuse me nothing.'

"'Beware how you speak the name of my wife again!' I said, 'or I will throw you through that window.'

"'Your wife?' said he. 'Nonsense, my good fellow! I married the woman myself five years ago; we have never been divorced; and her little escapade with you does not alter her legal relation to me.'

CHAPTER XII.

A TALE OF THE CITY.

AT this point in his story, General Weymouth paused and turned his gaze from the fire to Kitty Clive's face. He saw tears in her eyes ; and as he looked they ran down her cheeks. She did not seem to be aware of them. There was profound sympathy and compassion in her regard ; and he was the more sensible thereof because she made no attempt to put her feeling into words.

"I have sometimes asked myself," the general presently continued, "and I have never found an entirely satisfactory answer to the question, whether it would not have been a wise and meritorious act on my part to have killed that man then and there. I came within a hair's-breadth of doing it ; and I can not say that I have been glad that I refrained. But almost immediately the thought came, 'What he says is false,' and I determined to prove it. All I said to him was, 'I will accompany you to my home, and you can then repeat what you have just told me. I advise you to say nothing more to me in the meanwhile.'

"He shrugged his shoulders. We went out together and got into a horse-car to go up town. Be-

fore we started, I took a revolver out of my drawer
and put it in the pocket of my overcoat. I kept
my hand upon it during the journey, intending to
shoot him if he made any attempt to escape. But
he did not attempt it. At last we reached my
home. I opened the door with a latch-key, and we
entered the hall. The drawing-room was on the
left. I heard my wife at the piano. I motioned
the fellow to stay in the hall, while I went in. My
wife looked round, and ran from the piano with an
exclamation of surprise and pleasure. She had not
expected me back for several hours. She came
forward with her arms outstretched, to kiss me.
As I looked at her, I felt certain that the story was
a lie. I took her in my arms and kissed her. It '
was the last kiss I ever gave her.

" She asked me what brought me back so soon
I told her that a man had been at my office who
asserted that he had been acquainted with her,
that I believed him to be a swindler, and that, in
order to settle the matter, I had told him I would
ask her.

" I was holding her affectionately by the arms. I
felt her arms grow rigid in my hands. She turned
her face away for a moment ; then she looked
straight at me, smiling, and said, ' What is his
name ? '

" ' He has two,' I answered ; and I told her what
they were.

" She turned pale, and moistened her lips. She
stepped back, removing herself from my embrace,

and chafing the back of one hand with the palm of the other. She said in a dry voice, 'Oh, he is an impostor. It's impossible. I never heard of him.'

"I turned to the door and called out, 'Come in here!'

"He came in. When she saw him, her face changed till it looked like death; then her eyes all at once shone like fire, and she leaped towards him as if she meant to kill him. But she did not reach him; she stopped, shaking all over, and gave a wild scream, half laughing, and with some words in it that I could not distinguish, and staggered and dropped on the floor. I have seen men who were killed in battle die just like that.

"'You see I told you the truth,' said the fellow.

"'Yes,' I said. 'Tell me the rest.'

"He told me the story. He had met the girl; her father was a disreputable man, and he was using her as a bait to catch a rich husband. This fellow ruined the girl; but her father induced him to marry her, and employ her as a sort of stool-pigeon in various kinds of infamous transactions. At last the crime was planned and carried out which resulted in the arrest and conviction of the husband. The woman went back to her father. They agreed that since the husband was dead to all practical intents and purposes—put out of the way for fifteen years—she should resume her maiden name and try to get another husband. The scheme was put in operation, and after three years they succeeded in entrapping me. 'Now,' said the fellow in con-

clusion, 'you may keep her if you want her; I
have no use for her. But you are a highly respected
gentleman, with the best possible social connections.
You want to keep this affair quiet; you don't want
to be mixed up in any bigamy proceedings. Business is business. I have my living to make. If I
am to hold my tongue, I shall look to you for
funds. So long as they are forthcoming, that
woman may call herself Mrs. Weymouth to her
heart's content. But as soon as you repudiate my
drafts, or expose me in any way, or oppose me in
any plans I attempt to carry out, I shall claim my
wife through the courts, and the whole yarn will
appear in the papers. What are you going to do?"

"I said, 'I shall protect this lady, who has been
known by my name, and who probably married me
in the belief that you were dead. I will pay you a
reasonable yearly sum to keep out of our way.
You will do wisely not to try me too far. That's all
I have to tell you.'

"He said, 'You will find my address on the card
I gave you. I shall expect a check for ten thousand dollars to reach me there by noon to-morrow.
Otherwise, I shall begin proceedings the next
morning.'

"He went out, and I was left alone with her. I
lifted her from the floor and carried her to the
sofa. She recovered consciousness in a few minutes.
I sat beside her, as she lay there, and we had a
talk, in which arrangements were made for the
future. We were gradually to cease to visit or re-

ceive friends. We were to occupy the same house
while in town ; but she was to go to some country
place during the summer, while I would remain in
New York on plea of business. Little by little we
would separate more and more. I requested her
to refrain from any thing likely openly to dishonor
my name ; and I on my side would do all I could
to protect her from suspicion or insult. If she had
loved me," said the General, after a pause, " I
would have acted in another manner. I would have
defied her husband, and, as we could not legally
be man and wife,—I would have taken her to
another country and lived with her there, a husband
to her before God if not by the law of man. But
she did not love me ; she could not even pretend
that she did ; and therefore she could not have
been content under any such arrangement. As for
me, I had loved her with all my heart at first ;
and if I did not love her after that discovery it
was because my heart was dead. But I could not
abandon her ; I could not but do my utmost to protect her against herself. God knows, that although
I let it be understood that my course was prompted
by a desire to shield my family name and my
honor, my real motive was only to be kind to her.
Ah, poor girl—poor girl ! "

His eyes were again bent upon the fire, as if he
saw there the glowing youthful beauty of the woman
through whom his life had been wrecked. By and
by he roused himself and continued.

" I had no intention of speaking to you so fully

of these things," he said ; " but I have allowed myself to run on, and, in excuse, I may ·say that you
are the. first human being, my dear Miss Clive, to
whom I have ever spoken of this episode of my
life.   I have told it to you because I felt impelled
to do so ; I knew that you would respect my confidence and understand my feeling.   And I also had
another object, which I will now explain.

" After the first shock was over, I made up my
mind not to let my calamity crush me.   As there
was no place for me at home, I set myself to making a home in the midst of affairs ; and my original crusade upon corruption and incompetence in
politics was taken up with all the added energy
that comes from a desire to escape from one's self.
But I met with an opposition upon which I had
not counted.

" The fellow who had come across my path—I
will call him Fowler—had received large sums of
money from me, and had entered into what are
called politics.   He was shrewd and supple, and
utterly unprincipled.   He used his ill-gotten money
with good effect, and advanced himself with wonderful rapidity.   Such men can make themselves very
useful to bigger men, who do not care to inquire
into the character of their henchmen, if they can
attain their ends through them.   Fowler realized,
as I had done, the almost unlimited power of the
great financiers ; but he plotted to get that power
on his own side; and in supporting it, to aggrandize

himself. He began to be recognized as a powerful and able fellow.

"A short time before this, I had become acquainted with Maxwell Golding. He is a man who has made his own way and possesses remarkable traits of character. I did not like the system he represented, or the methods he adopted ; but I liked him. He was in earnest, he was patient, he had far-reaching views, he could plan vast enterprises, and, if any unexpected conditions arose, he could alter his plans so as to meet the new situation. He has the mind of a great commander and statesman, but he cares little for name and fame ; he regards the reality of power more than to see his power recognized ; and he is convinced that the most real power in modern civilization is money. He professes small belief in human virtue and honor ; but his own private life is blameless, and he never departs from his own code of business morality. From one point of view he is a merciless brigand ; from another, he is a man who simply takes things and men as he finds them and makes them the instruments of his designs. But after all is said, there is a personal fascination about the man, which I have felt, and which I believe to be at the bottom of some of his most remarkable successes. It is a cold sort of fascination, and he does not seem to exercise it consciously ; but it binds men to him, and makes them anxious to serve him, they know not why.

"I was frank in stating my aims to Golding—

that I wished to do away with the class to which he belonged as a political and economic factor in the country. He listened to my arguments, and assented to many of them ; but the only argument he used was, ' You can't stop it. It is natural, here and now, that money should be a power. I have money and I mean to use it.' The morality of his use of capital, or its ultimate effects upon the welfare of the nation, he would not discuss. ' I'm not a sentimentalist,' he said. ' Nations are not made of paper constitutions and declarations, but of men and women. We may pretend to be or to profess any thing ; but we are nothing but so many men and women, when all's done ; and we propose each to do the best he can for himself.' At the same time he had no objection to my opposing him and what he represented to the utmost of my ability. ' You are right enough in the abstract,' he said ; ' and if you think you can realize your theories, go ahead ! '

"Well, my dear young lady, I went ahead with all the strength I had. The money which Fowler took from me hampered me somewhat, and I had settled a hundred thousand dollars on my wife (as I must call her) in such a manner that she could touch only the interest of it. I bought a newspaper and used it to inculcate my views. I made every effort to push the paper ; and for a time it was favorably received by the public. But by and by I became convinced that an enemy was working against me. I could not see him, I could not touch him, but I was aware of him at every point. His attacks were subtle and made from twenty different directions, but they were all of the same character. They aimed at vital points—to discredit me socially, politically, ·personally. I found that people whom I had always regarded as staunch friends were inoculated with the poison. I tried to trace down the slanders and insinuations to their source, but in vain. I was like a man blindfold, striking at invisible assassins. At length one of the most powerful papers, commanding an immense circulation, began publishing a series of articles on the same subjects which I was treating in my paper. They purported to take the same ground that I did, but with differences, slight in appearance but vital in quality, that led to very alien conclusions. At the same time, there were transparently veiled allusions to my paper and myself, insinuating doubts as to the integrity and disinterestedness of my aims. The effect of all this was first to forestall and pervert my arguments, and then to discredit me as a journalist and a man ; yet all was done with such cunning and seeming candor, as to sound like impersonal zeal for the public welfare. I did what I could, and spent what I had, but in spite of all, the circulation of my paper decreased every day, and advertisers fell off. I was obstinate, for I believed I was in the right, and that right would prevail ; I executed a mortgage on the paper, and laid out most of the money in renewed efforts to extend its circulation ;

but the tide continued to set steadily against me. When the mortgage fell due I tried to get it renewed. But I discovered that it had been bought up by some other person ; this person foreclosed, and I was bankrupt. On that day I received a letter from Fowler, avowing that it was he who had been secretly acting against me all along, and who had now for the second time accomplished my ruin. This letter enlightened me as to various obscure points in the past. I went to see Golding.

" He received me alone in his private office. I began to tell him that I had fought to the end, and had been defeated, but he interrupted me. ' I know all about it,' he said. ' I told you, if you thought you could succeed, to go ahead ; but you have had a practical lesson that money can do more than abstract morality. It was I who fought you and beat you. I used the methods that are customary in such cases, and they were effectual, as they always are. Neither you nor any man can make way against them.'

" ' And you have employed this fellow Fowler— my personal enemy, a wretch——'

" ' I know nothing about Fowler's relations with you,' he interrupted me, ' and I have made no inquiries as to his private character. He was the sort of person I needed for the job, and I employed him. He did his work well, and has been well paid for it. If you want to put a bullet through him, or prosecute him for libel, you are welcome to do it. I have no further concern about him. But

I have something else to suggest, which I think
will suit you better.'

" ' What is it ?' I asked.

" Then he unfolded to me his scheme of a great
industrial enterprise, to be controlled secretly by
himself, but ostensibly by a board of managers ;
and of this board he offered me the presidency.
' I make you the offer,' he said, ' partly to show
you that I have no personal feeling against you,
and that I wish you well, and that in this fight I
have attacked what you stand for, and not you ;
and if you got hurt, it was because you stood up
too obstinately. But the chief reason for my offer
is that you are the man most suitable for the position. Your name, in spite of the innuendos that
have been thrown upon it, is still of great influence,
and will gain the confidence of the kind of people
we wish to get hold of. I have calculated that
your help will be worth fifty thousand a year to me,
and that will be the amount of your salary. The
main lines of the policy to be pursued will be laid
down by me ; but you will have full liberty as regards details. You can do a great deal of good in
your own way—more than you will ever be able to
do otherwise. Do you accept ?'

" ' No,' I said, ' I can not accept it.'

" ' Remember,' he said, ' that I am not inviting
you out of friendship. I don't consider that I owe
you any reparation or apology for having defeated
and ruined you. We are both soldiers, in our different ways, and all is fair in war. I invite you

for practical business reasons. Your name and reputation will be useful to me. If it were not so —if you were unknown or forgotten—I would not offer you so much as a clerkship at twenty dollars a month—not if you were the Angel Gabriel, and had saved my life. There is the offer, to take or leave. You will never get such a chance again. Think of all it implies. Come, General, oblige me !—take it ! '

"I felt at that moment how strong and almost irresistible he was. He was offering to pay me for the honest reputation which I should betray by taking his money, and yet, instead of being angry, it was all I could do to refrain from yielding to him. But I did refrain ; and when he saw that I was firm, he smiled, and ceased to urge me. 'I'm sorry,' he said, ' but you will gain nothing by your refusal, except poverty and your own self-satisfaction. I shall get another man, as like you as possible, to fill the place you might have had. That's all. I'm busy. Good-by, Weymouth."

" ' Good-by,' I said, and I walked out ; and I have not seen Golding since then, until to-day. And so, at last, Miss Clive, in a very roundabout way, I come to the point of my story.

"I went to him this morning. He recognized me at once, and greeted me as if we had parted but a day before. I told him that I had been living during the past years in retirement and on very limited means ; but that latterly circumstances had arisen which made me desire to secure a larger income. I told him that I had become deeply and tenderly interested in a young lady "—here the General's voice grew deeper and gentler—"and that although I was no longer young, but an old and broken man, I should make bold to ask her to be my wife. I said that I came to him as to the largest employer of labor in America, and therefore the man most likely to have positions at his disposal. Would he give me something to do?

"He said : ' The last time I saw you I offered you a place worth fifty thousand a year.'

" 'You did,' I answered : 'but you asked too much in return for the money.'

" ' That may be true,' he said. ' I always try to get the best of a bargain. Well, you refused it, and that is the end of it, isn't it ?'

" ' I had no thought of any position of that kind; my requirements will be very small,' I told him.

" He looked at me for a few moments, and then said, " I can do nothing for you, Weymouth. You come to me on a matter of business, and I answer you as a business man. You have been living in retirement for ten years or more. You have become entirely forgotten. Except for your honorable reputation for integrity and high principle, you never were worth any thing in practical affairs. As I told you long ago, it was for your reputation for integrity and high principle that I was willing to pay. But now that you and your reputation · have lapsed into oblivion, you are worth nothing at all to me. I don't say it harshly, or with any feel-

ing one way or the other ; I only tell you a fact.
And if I wanted to advise you I should say, Don't
get married, and don't try, at your age, to begin
any new employment.'

"I said nothing, but got up to go. 'Wait a
moment,' he said. 'Now that the business part of
our interview is over, I am free to talk to you as
between man and man. I always liked you, Weymouth, and I believe you are a good fellow, though
your theories and schemes for improving the condition of things are all wrong and foolish. If you
will accept a hundred thousand dollars from me
as a free gift, you are welcome to have it.' He
opened a check-book and added, 'Say the word,
and here it is !'

"I can't put myself under an obligation to you,"
I told him.

"'Well, then,' he said, 'I'll make out the check
to the lady you want to marry. What is her
name?'

"'Not that, either,' I answered, 'I do not know
whether she would have me for her husband ; and
if she did I could not ask her to accept money in
that way.'

"'Very well,' he said, 'that's all I can do,'—and
so, Miss Clive," added the General, "I left him,
and here I am. I see, now, that I have acted fool-
ishly throughout. But I loved you, and I wished
to add something to your life ; and I thought that
if I could make an income sufficient to support
you in comfort you would perhaps consent to let

the close of my life be brightened and sweetened by your companionship. It would have been happiness to me to work for you, or to do anything for you. But love made a fool of me ; and I should be glad rather than sorry that my mission to Golding was a failure. It saves you the pain of saying that you can not care for me. You must forgive me for having indulged myself in the luxury of telling you, in words as well as by behavior and implication, that I love you and shall always love you. That other love was not like this ; it was of the eye, not of the mind and soul." He paused a moment, and then said, " She died a year ago."

CHAPTER XIII.

OUT OF JOINT.

" I NEVER expected to hear such words from
any man as you have spoken to me, General Weymouth," said Kitty. " I am not a girl that
men fall in love with. I am liked, not loved. You
are the only man that has ever loved me, and I am
proud to know that a man like you can give me his
love. It makes me feel that I am not apart from
other women, as I fancied myself to be before.
But I can not marry you, dear General Weymouth ;
I shall never marry any one."

" You are too young to say ' never,' " returned
the General, with a sad smile.

" Not young in the sense you mean," she said.
" I have not had the usual life of a young woman
of my station. I have not always met with kind-
ness or with justice. My mother died early, and
my father's second wife was my enemy. I never
told him of her conduct to me, because he thought
her perfection, and I would not undeceive him ;
but, if I kept my thoughts and feelings to myself,
I thought and felt them all the more deeply ; and
they were not all of the kind that are supposed to

belong to Christian children. I am not a Christian, General Weymouth."

" The creed is not every thing," he replied. " You are good, and generous, and high-minded."

" I am good and generous to those who are so to me ; but I do not forgive those who do me evil. And that is not all ; for, since you have given me your confidence, you have a right to mine. I believe in retaliation and in maintaining your rights by violence, if fair means will not do. If I had been in your place, I would not have acted as you did."

" If there was any magnanimity in my acts, they were what yours would have been."

"No !" she said, with an emphasis that her interlocutor was hardly prepared for. " No ; I am not magnanimous ! Let those who are secure and prosperous be so ! I would have defied that man and challenged him to do his worst. But I would have made myself more terrible to him than he was to me. I would have hunted him through the world, and made his life worse than death to him. I would have found out what he the most cared for —every human being cares for something—and I would have struck him through that, as he struck at you. I would never have relented or spared him one suffering that I could inflict. What is your name, your social standing, any thing, compared with the pleasure of making those who have wronged you curse the day when they first crossed your path ? And as for that woman who deceived

you, she was more unpardonable than he ! Only a
woman can realize the wickedness that that woman
perpetrated. You should have cast her off pub-
licly and unconditionally. You should have driven
her out of society and out of the world ! Why, see
what results your weakness caused—your merci-
fulness and magnanimity, if such it be ! The man,
your enemy, with the money he had extorted from
you, hounded you out of your public career, and
prevented all the good that your principles, put in
practice, would have accomplished. Was that
worth while, for the sake of sparing a worthless
creature who never had a thought or an emotion
that was not base and selfish ? And this man
Golding, whom you find so nearly irresistible—I
would be no friend of him either. He is strong,
but depend upon it there are weak points in his
armor too ! You should have fought him to
death, with every weapon that ingenuity or desper-
ation could devise. There should be no half
measures in this life ; its rewards, such as they are,
belong only to those who realize that it is all a
battle, and who throw themselves into it body,
heart, and soul. These gentle, forgiving ways are
good to write of in books, but they never bring
about any thing that is real and can last. Who is
Mr. Golding that you should submit to be defeated
by him ? How should he dare to treat a man like
you with good-natured contempt, as he did this
morning ? You allow him to do it ; and you are
to blame ! "

The general was silenced and amazed by this passionate and destructive criticism. He had been aware that Kitty Clive had pregnant depths in her character, but he little imagined what strange things were to be found beneath the surface. He felt the force and poignancy of many of her declarations, but he also felt that they were the outcome of quite another mind and temperament than his, and that he could never hope to adopt them himself. Be that as it might, he was conscious that the mental stature of the woman had immensely expanded to his apprehension within the last few minutes; and his love for her underwent a corresponding development. He had heretofore regarded her as a girl possessed of a nature rich in quality and of great possibilities; now he saw her a woman of original thought and experience, who had worked out her own convictions of what life meant and needed, and had the courage and ability to act up to them. To stand in the most intimate relation to such a being as this would be something more than mere happiness; it would be exhilaration and elevation. He looked at her with kindling eyes.

"Why do you say that you will never marry?" he demanded.

"I will tell you," she answered; "but I tell it to you alone, and it must never be told again. I will marry no one, because I can not marry the man I love."

"You love some one, then?" the General bent

his head to hide the twinge of the heart that was made visible in his face. Presently he looked up and added, " Why can't you marry him ? "

" Because he doesn't know that I love him ; and, even if he did, he would never love me."

" Can it be possible ! " returned the General. " You love him—and he doesn't love you ! Can it be possible ! "

" And so you have your revenge," she added with a quaint smile.

" My dear Miss Clive, my happiness does not lie in revenges. If I could bring about your marriage with this gentleman—he must be worthy since you care for him—I am sure I would do it. There can not be any thing more than some accidental blindness—some pre-occupation that the least hint would remove—that delays him from falling at your feet."

" If his blindness were only physical and per-manent," returned Kitty, with a laugh, " I should have better hopes. But it is not every man, General Weymouth, who can forget the outside in looking at what is within. Besides, this gentleman is a distant cousin of mine, and the familiarities of cousinship—well, it is like a child eating too much bread before dinner ; he becomes indifferent. But, after all, it doesn't matter ; it is better as it is. I would rather imagine what marriage might be than risk proving what it is. If he were to love and marry me, and then become tired of me—ah ! then ! "

The last words were spoken below her breath,

but with an emphasis that left nothing unexpressed.

"That could never be. He might never awaken to what you are ; but, having done so, he could never fall back again," said the General, with conviction.

"Oh, yes ; you don't realize how ugly I am ; and you don't know how jealous and despotic I should be—as a wife. It is better as it is ; I have no rights, and can therefore claim none. My love can be wholly unselfish. It is sweet to know that it will always be a secret from him. He will feel the effects, and yet never know whence they come. In many ways I can give him happiness ; and to see him happy will be better than any gratitude he could render to me. I am content with my state. Beautiful women have their power, their triumph, but it is a shallow one. It is a house built upon sand. The winds and waters of time and chance will destroy it. There can be no such calamity in store for me. What there is of me is founded upon a rock, and can never be overthrown."

"I can do nothing, then," said the General, sadly.

"You have done a great deal. If a woman's heart were in her brain—and some women's are— life would be much more comfortable. I can recognize, with my brain, that you are more worthy of love than this man who does not love me. He might speak with more passion than you ; but he could not express such depth and nobility of affection—he could not feel it ! Yes, I can see that he

is not worthy of such love as I give him ; but who is
worthy of love ?   It is something divine and in-
finite, coming through us mortal and finite
creatures, but not of us.   I am no more worthy of
your love than he of mine ; but it glorifies me to
know that I have it, and gives me more strength to
—forgive me—to love him ! ''

" That feels cruel," said the General, drawing his
breath between his teeth with a little gasp, " but I
know that it is true—and kind."   He rose to his
feet, and glanced here and there about the room.
" As to those radical opinions of yours, my dear -
child," he added, in a more composed tone, " they
are not vital nor lasting.   The strands of your
nature have been twisted awry, and the harmony is
broken for a time.   But the truth and goodness in
you are stronger than any evil influence and will
finally prevail.   You can not make your own rights
and wrongs the criterion of the justice of God's
universe.   All tragedies are partial and frag-
mentary.   The longer the arc of experience, the
more does sunshine prevail in it."

" Shall you stop coming to see me because of
this ?" Kitty asked.

" Not unless you wish it," he replied.   " I can not
be cured by absence, and I can promise you that
you shall not be harassed by regrets and entreaties.
I feel that your attitude towards me is final."

" Then come often," she said, giving him her
hand.   " Perhaps I shall be worthier of your friendship if I know that I possess it,"

When the General had gone Kitty sat down at her piano and touched the chords and sang. She sang without words, as the wind sings in the Æolian harp ; but the rise and fall and changes of her voice expressed her mood to herself as only music can express it. And perhaps a great composer, listening to her, might have divined more of the secrets of her heart and soul than any human speech, even her own, could have told him.

In the course of an hour, Frank Cunliffe came in. She did not leave the piano, but turned her head and smiled a greeting to him over her shoulder, while her fingers still wandered over the keys.

"You always seem to be enjoying yourself." Frank remarked, as he threw himself down in a chair near her. "Nothing ever troubles you or depresses you. I believe a little misery would do you good."

"No misery amounts to any thing, if your digestion is right and your circulation in good order," she answered. "Eating, sleeping, and exercise make happiness."

"Ah ! that's all you know. I wish you could have some desperate love-affair, or lose your voice, or something."

"Why, what now, cousin ?" she said, still playing with the keys. "Is it you who are in love at last ? or is it still your lost income that you are lamenting ? "

"I wish you'd let that piano alone and be sensible," he exclaimed, with an aggrieved air. "You are becoming quite frivolous!"

"Would you have me shiver at the Equator, or perspire at the Pole? I am in Rome, and I am as the Romans are."

"If I am as the Romans, it must be at the period of the Decline and Fall," said Frank. "My position in the world has never been one of such brilliance that Fate need have grown envious of me; but it seems as if I had taken a turn and was to go downward from now on. It is not my digestion that disorders my affairs; it is my affairs that disorder my digestion."

"Has any thing new happened?" she asked, leaving the piano and going over to the fire-place, where she leaned with one arm on the mantel-piece.

"I don't know," he said. "I'm half inclined to think that something or other is going on, having me for its object; but I can't find out what it is, and perhaps it is only my morbid and bilious condition that puts it into my head. It's a nuisance, all the same."

"Something going on? What sort of a something?"

"Well, I have a notion that I am being followed or watched. I have heard that that is the way a man feels when he is going insane. It's the first symptom of melancholia. Have I committed some crime, without being aware of it? or am I watched to see whether I intend to commit one? or am I the victim of a new form of delirium tremens, derived from drinking the cup of mortification to the dregs ? I can't understand it."

" Nonsense, Frank ! Take a run round the block, and clear the cobwebs out of your brain ! who would want to follow you, or watch you either ? I never heard such a conceited idea ! "

" Oh, detectives don't follow one because he is beautiful or lovely."

" Detectives ! what next ? "

" Look out of the window."

Kitty laughed, walked across the room, and standing within the shadow of the curtain glanced up and down the street. A thaw had set in, the sidewalks were wet and sloppy, and the roadway a slough of dirty snow. A man, with his coat-collar turned up to his ears, and his hands thrust in his side-pockets, was plodding up the street. He was smoking a short pipe, and looked like a specimen of the American working-man out of a job. At the corner of the adjoining avenue there was a tobacco shop, the show-window of which was rendered gorgeous by the colored pictures of young women in airy costumes celebrating the virtues of nicotine. The man stopped in front of this window, and stood for a while in apparent admiration of its scenic dis-·play ; then, instead of passing onwards, he turned round and started back down the street. After having passed some distance beyond Kitty's window, he paused again, knocked the ashes out of his pipe against a lamp-post, and began hunting in his pockets as if for tobacco. None being forth-coming, he slowly retraced his steps to the tobac-conist's, and this time entered the shop. Kitty returned to the fire-place.

" Well, did you see any thing?" Frank inquired, looking up from a brown study.

" What I always see when I look out of window —the street, and people in it."

" One of those people is after me. I don't know which one it is, and I don't think it's always the same one ; but every once in a while I turn round, and meet the eyes of some one looking at me. He looks away immediately, and passes along, and that's the end of it ; but by and by, again, there is a pair of eyes looking at me. Yes, you may say it's imagination ; so I told myself at first ; but why was I never afflicted with this particular vagary of imagination before ?   I repeat, it's a nuisance."

" Have you committed any crime ?" asked Kitty, looking him in the face.

" No ; nothing worse than usual. But I shall, before long, if for no other reason, just to bring this mystery to a head, and find out what is at the bottom of it."

" Don't be uneasy, my dear boy," said Kitty, bending over him and laying her hand for a mo-ment on his shoulder. " I have a presentiment. that all will be well with you before long."

CHAPTER XIV.

IN THE WOODS.

"I FANCY you were right, Inspector," said Captain Hamilton, as the two sat in a retired restaurant down-town, partaking of a temperate luncheon. "There is nothing against Cowran, except his old quarrel with Golding, and that matter of the secret papers ; but neither of these is inconsistent with his entire innocence. On the contrary, if he had wanted to injure Golding he would unquestionably have published those papers ; and if he had wished to blackmail him he would have extorted money by the threat of publishing them."

"What reason for returning the papers does he put forward ? " the Inspector asked.

"A reason so commonplace that it seems unlikely so clever a man would have invented it. I mean that it's too commonplace not to be true."

"How did you induce him to give it ? "

"By taking up the thread of a former conversation I had with him about Golding. You recollect my telling you in what bitter and violent terms he had spoken of him ? Well, I found a pretext for introducing his name again, and remarked that I

thought he (Cowran) did him less than justice.
After a little talk, he said——"

"Give the conversation exactly as it occurred,"
interrupted Inspector Byrnes.

"Very well, sir.   Cowran replied to my remark
that of course I was at liberty to form my own
opinion ; and wanted to know who had been setting me right in the matter.

"I told him that my impression was at first hand.
I had been casually introduced to Golding by
a partner or business associate of his, Mr.
Courtlandt Owens, and had had a long chat with
him.

"'I don't say he can't make himself agreeable,'
Cowran said.   'He would be a much less dangerous man if he could not.'

"I said, 'So far as I was concerned, he was
simply polite, and nothing more.   I was thinking of
what he said of you.'"

"Cowran looked surprised and said, 'What did he
say of me ?'

"'Your name was mentioned—by Owens I
think—' said I, 'and Golding observed that he had
once known you well, and that you were a man of
great ability—that there was no better lawyer in
New York. But he said there had been a misunderstanding on your part about some action of
his on the street, and that you had quarreled with
him. It was when they had been bulling the price
of gold, and the government had suddenly bought
largely, and the price fell like a man out of a

balloon. Golding had to unload, and there was no time to go round and warn friends. 'He has never forgiven you,' said Owens. 'I am not sure about that, either,' said Golding, ' and I'll tell you why. At the time Cowran, as my confidential lawyer, had in his possession some documents belonging to me of a somewhat delicate character; I had forgotten that he had them, and nothing more was heard of them until a few days ago. Then I received them from him in a packet, by a special messenger. It was a courteous and considerate act.'

" ' That certainly doesn't look like bearing malice,' Owens said ; and then Golding went on and said a number of complimentary things about you. I had half a mind, just for fun, to tell him some of the remarks you had made about him a few days before ; but I didn't ! '

" Cowran listened to all that coolly, and gave a grunt, but said nothing ; so I added, ' I suppose you were putting up a joke on me, and didn't mean what you said. It isn't likely you'd do a man such a favor as that if you really thought ill of him.'

" ' I don't see any particular favor about it,' Cowran answered. ' It was just common honesty, neither more nor less. I happened to be thinking about that old lawsuit one day, and remembered the papers. I asked my clerk about them, and he said they were in the deed-box. I got them out, had copies made of them, and sent the originals to him. They belonged to him, and I had no use for them.'

' Then what did you want of a copy, of them?' I asked. ' As a matter of record and protection, of course,' he said. ' Golding might say that they had come into my possession unlawfully ; but the copy proves that I received them at a time and in circumstances which preclude any such possibility.' That was his story," added Captain Hamilton: "and for my part I don't see any more natural way of explaining it."

" Was his manner as natural as his explanation ? " demanded the Inspector.

" Every bit ; that was the most convincing part of it."

" What have you done about Cunliffe ? "

" I have made out a very strong presumption against him ; not enough to convict, by any means, but enough to work on for a conviction. It seems he lost a lot of money a month or more ago, speculating in Golding stocks."

" You are certain of that ? "

" Yes ; I have it from his brokers. It was about twenty thousand. It must have been pretty nearly all he had,"

" Does he consider Golding responsible for it ? "

" I fancy he thinks Golding could make it good without inconvenience," was the reply.

" Is that all ? "

" No ; that is only a plausible motive. It is strengthened by the fact that he is on terms of close friendship with a girl—an opera singer or something of that kind—whom he brought out and started on her career. So far as can be learned, there is nothing against her private character ; so that, supposing him to contemplate marriage, he would have double need of money :—at least double ! " added the captain, with an arch smile.

" The fact that he speculated also works that way," commented the Inspector. " If he is not in the habit of it, he is likely to have had some special reason ; and the prospect of getting married would be urgent enough."

" Well, then," continued the captain, " here is the other fact. On the day before that letter was written referring to the secret papers, Cunliffe spent the evening at John Talbot's house ; and Miss Claverhouse, the type-writer at Cowran's, was there too. She had made the copy of the papers that very day ; and it is at least possible that she, being a rather talkative young person, may have let fall enough to give Cunliffe the hint that the letter contained. That comes in rather neatly, I think ! "

" It is well pieced together," said the Inspector, musingly ; " and yet, somehow, it doesn't give me the feeling I sometimes have of being certainly on the right track. The tone and style of these letters are difficult to reconcile with either Cowran or Cunliffe. They would have disguised themselves, of course ; but they would have done it, to my way of thinking, in some other way. Does Cunliffe still seem to be in a depressed state financially ? "

" As to his financial state, I can only speak of

his transactions with his brokers.   But he certainly appears very low-spirited."

"We know, however, that the author of the letters has twice speculated successfully on Golding's recommendation," the Inspector said. " The information was given to him through the press in the terms of the cipher he selected, and he has written expressing his acknowledgments. If Cunliffe is the man, he ought to have cheered up a little."

" He has been shadowed constantly," Hamilton went on, " but has not been seen either to post any letters or to go near Wall Street."

" Mind you don't overdo the shadowing business," the Inspector said.   " Unless I am mistaken in him, he is very observant and sensitive, and if he were to suspect that he was being followed all would go for nothing.   Besides, if he did post a letter, it would prove nothing, unless we know whom it was addressed to.   As for his not visiting Wall Street, or any broker's office in town, for that matter, I know it already ; my arrangements were such that if the speculations in Golding's stocks had been executed in this city, I should have been informed of it, and would have had the means of tracing the operator."

"He knew enough to do his work out of town, then ?"

" Evidently."

" Well, he's a clever fellow.   But wouldn't it be possible to get sight of the addresses on the letters (assuming that Cunliffe is the man we want) before he posted them ? "

" Possible no doubt," said the Inspector, shruging his shoulders.

" He must write them either at the club or in his own rooms," resumed the other ; "and in either case he probably dries the writing with blotting-paper. Now, the address on the envelope is generally the last thing written, and a man blots it immediately, before putting on the stamp. I have the run of the club, and though I have never been up to Cunliffe's rooms, I could get there without much trouble. If I could find a single piece of blotting-paper with Golding's name on it, the thing would be as good as settled."

" There is something in that notion," the Inspector said, " and it has sometimes been tried successfully—especially in novels. But Mr. Cunliffe probably reads novels, and may burn his blotting-paper as soon as he has used it, or he may write the letters at a hotel, or at the office of an acquaintance —perhaps of a man who has some relations with Golding himself, or it may happen that Cunliffe is one of those men who guard against all remote and unlikely contingencies, and don't allow for the obvious ones under their noses ; and in that case your plan might catch him. We have tried a good many ways now, and nothing has succeeded. Unless we mean to give up and admit ourselves beaten, we must hit upon something before long. Before many days it will be too late."

" How so, Inspector?"

" The fellow will have got all he can venture to
take, and have cleared out.   He has probably set
out to net a certain sum, and when he has obtained
it he will quit.   He knows the danger he is running, since he threw off the mask and appeared in
his true colors as a blackmailer.   We may find out
at any moment, by any accident, through whom he
does his business, and then he is lost.   He will
quit, the letters will stop, and we shall never know
who he is.   That will never do ! "

" How would it do to invite him off on a trip somewhere—to the Hot Sulphur Springs, say—and
keep him under my eye all the time.   It could be
arranged so that we would occupy the same room
and be constantly together.   During that time——"

" During that time," the Inspector interposed,
" aud supposing Cunliffe to be the man, Mr. Golding would probably not receive any of the letters."

The Captain handled his whiskers.   " At all
events," he said at length, " it might prove a negative.   If Mr. Golding did receive a letter during
that time, we should know that Cunliffe didn't
write it."

" It might be tried with this addition," the Inspector remarked, after a moment's thought.   " During your trip with him, we might insert in the paper
an advertisement so worded as to demand an immediate answer.   He would be obliged either to
answer it or to miss an important opportunity.
The few hours during which his answer must be

written would be the limit of the time you would have to watch him. And it would be enough if you even saw him post a letter, without knowing any thing about the address of it ; for if Golding received a letter next day bearing the post-mark of the town you were staying in—it would be an awkward coincidence for Mr. Cunliffe ! "

" I believe you have hit it at last, Inspector ! " exclaimed Captain Hamilton, his eyes sparkling. "That must fetch him—there's no way out of it ! "

" There are two ways out of it," returned the Inspector, impassibly.

" What are they ? "

" The first is that if Cunliffe is not the man the plan will come to nothing. The second is that if he is the man——"

" Well, what then ? "

" Then he will refuse to leave New York in your company, or in fact to leave it at all."

Hamilton's face fell. The objection was well taken, and there seemed to be no escape from it.

" Never mind," said the Inspector, kindly, " though we haven't yet hit upon an infallible method, I think we have got upon the right track. The solution must be somewhere in this direction, if it's anywhere. Follow up that line, and by and by you will get there. And when you do, depend upon it it will be so simple you will wonder you never thought of it before."

"What shall I be doing in the meanwhile?" Hamilton inquired.

"I would go and hear that young lady sing, if I were you," replied the Inspector, arising from the table and putting on his hat.

CHAPTER XV.

BOLTED.

IT was Cunliffe's habit to appear at the club about ten o'clock every morning, having taken his breakfast of coffee and eggs in his rooms. Like a confirmed club man, his movements gradually became so adjusted to one another that any one familiar with him could have predicted where he could be found morning, noon, and night. Men of idle lives, who live in one place, are more apt to be regular in this way then men of affairs, though the springs that control them are so different.

Captain Hamilton, therefore, when he sauntered into the smoking-room at half-past ten, and, having summoned the waiter by a touch upon the electric bell-knob, had ordered a cigar and a cherry-soda—the Captain, I say, was so assured that Cunliffe was sitting in the second window from the door, reading the papers, that it was several moments before he turned in that direction to exchange a passing salute with him. When he did so, he saw only a vacant chair. Cunliffe had not yet arrived.

The Captain, after casting an exploring glance round the room, to discover whether his young

friend had perchance emigrated to. some other
quarter, seated himself in the vacant chair as
locum tenens ; and when the waiter came with the
soda and cigars he asked him, as he struck a match,
whether Mr. Cunliffe were not late that morning.

"Yes, sir," replied the man ; "it's an unusual
thing for Mr. Cunliffe, too. He'd ought to have
been here half an hour ago."

The Captain made up his mind that he had over-
slept himself, as even the idlest of young men
about town sometimes will, and resigned himself
to wait for him. He had been turning over in his
mind the consultation with the Inspector of the
day previous, and had come to the conclusion that
it could do no harm to at least propose a little trip
to Cunliffe, and see how he received the proposition.
If he rejected it, without giving any satisfactory
reasons, it would be a point against him, though
not, of course, a conclusive one. If he accepted it
readily and without embarrassment, the Captain
could use his own judgment as to going or raising
some obstacle at the last moment.

The smoking-room was far from being a disagreeable place to spend a vacant hour in. The
morning sunshine fell slantwise through its windows,
and the white illumination from the snow-covered
avenue was reflected into the apartment. At each
end of the room a genial fire was glowing and
blazing in an ample fireplace ; and at the various
little round tables well-dressed men were sitting in

easy chairs, chatting with one another in that
subdued tone which distinguishes the morning club-
man from the same personage after dinner. All
was warm, sumptuous, and serene; and the
sense of comfort was enhanced by the spectacle of
the bright frosty weather out-doors, where the
pedestrians walked with quickened steps along the
ringing sidewalks, and held their hands over their
ears, while their breath blew from their mouths
like puffs of thin white smoke.

The Captain sipped his soda and smoked his
cigar, and gave perfunctory attention to the newspaper that lay across his knee. Whenever any new-
comer entered the rooms, he looked up to see if it
were Cunliffe. His chair was so placed in the
window that he also commanded an outlook down
the avenue, and he kept an eye open for the
approach of his friend in that direction. But
eleven o'clock came and went, and still no Cunliffe.
The Captain finished his cigar, and debated whether
to light another. He decided the question in the
negative; he was not an excessive smoker, and
cigars were only a part of his professional
equipment. At half-past eleven he rose from his
chair, shook out first one leg and then the other,
stretched his arms, yawned, and walked over to the
fireplace.

"Hullo, Hamilton," said some one, from the
depths of an easy chair near by, "is that you? I
took it for granted you must be Cunliffe, sitting in
that window."

"By the by, where is Cunliffe?" the Captain asked.

"No idea: ought to be around here somewhere."

"Cunliffe?" came from another easy chair on the other side of the fireplace. "He won't be here to-day, I guess. Met him on the way up here. Said he was going out of town, I think. Had a valise."

"Confound the fellow!" ejaculated the Captain, rubbing his whiskers, "he had an appointment with me this morning. Did he say where he was going?"

"I don't know. I think not. I didn't ask him. He seemed rather in a hurry. Jumped aboard a horse-car."

"Humph! He's a nice chap, to leave me in the lurch this way!" the Captain growled. "Well, I can't wait any longer. If he should happen to come in, and any of you fellows see him, just tell him I waited an hour, will you?" And with the air of one who has been rudely entreated, the Captain strode out.

Inwardly, however, his emotions were much more active and acute than appeared in outward manifestation. The state of his mind, indeed, could be best described as one of consternation. If Cunliffe had bolted, there must have been some pressing reason for his doing so. Club men do not take trips out of New York in the dead of winter and the height of the season without grave cause. And the departure was as sudden as it was unusual. Hamilton had seen him the evening before, and

nothing in his manner or his words had indicated
that he had any such design in view.

Of course, his flight was the strongest possible
indication of his guilt. There were two ways of
regarding the event. Either he had got all the
money he wanted, and had made his preparations
deliberately ; or else he had been alarmed, and had
bolted at short warning to escape arrest. In either
case, the question was, where had he gone ? He
had at least two hours start. It was to be feared
that the pursuit would be too late, even if it could
be begun immediately.

But it was first necessary to make inquiries.
Upon leaving the club, Hamiliton betook himself
southward and westward to Cunliffe's lodgings.
Upon entering the street, he saw a man lingering
along the sidewalk, with his hands thrust up the
sleeves of his coat, and his head low down in his
collar. The man approached him, touching his hat,
and otherwise conducting himself after the manner
of the street-beggars who make club men their
prey. Hamilton walked along with an aspect of
studied unconsciousness ; meanwhile this conversation occurred :—

Hamilton.—What are you here for ?

Beggar.—Watchin' out for that feller, sir.

Hamilton.—Don't you know he's skipped?
When did you come here ?

Beggar.—Seven o'clock, sir. He ain't been out
since I been here.

Hamilton.—According to my information, he's

gone.   I will inquire at the house.   If he's not in,
I'll take out my handkerchief, and do you go down
and report at the office.   If he is, stay here.

Beggar.—All right, sir.

Then Hamilton, with the air of one who submits
to extortion for the sake of peace and quiet handed
the beggar a coin ; thereupon the latter touched
his hat again, turned on his heel, and walked off.

Hamilton ran up the steps of Cunliffe's lodgings
and rang the bell.   After a long delay, and just as
he was on the point of ringing again, the door was
opened by a female, who presented a countenace of
preternatural stupidity.

" Mr. Cunliffe in ?" demanded Hamilton, briskly.

The woman gazed at him with lack-luster eyes
for several moments, and then said, " Mr. What ? "

" Cunliffe—Mr. Frank Cunliffe—is he in ? "

" Mr. Cunliffe," repeated the girl, and stopped
to consider.   " No," she said at length, staring at
the Captain's necktie as if under the impression
that she had seen it somewhere before.   " No, he
ain't in—Mr. Cunliffe."

" Not in ?   That's odd !   Did he leave any word
for Captain Hamilton ? "

" Captain Hamilton ?   Who's he ? "

" I am Captain Hamilton.   Did he leave any
message or note for me ? "

" No ; he didn't leave nothing for nobody."

" What time did he go away ? "

The girl shook her head slowly.   " I don' know.
This mornin', I guess.   I didn't see him."

"Well, see here; can I step up to his room for a moment? I'm a friend of his, you know, and expected to find him here—important business—and just write a note for him. Just let me up to his room, will you?"

"Can't do it," said the girl, still shaking her head. "He's locked the door, and took the key off with him."

"Oh, the deuce he has! Where's the mistress of the house!"

"She's gone marketin'."

By this time the door was nearly closed; and with the final words it was clapped together with a bang, and the Captain was left out in the cold.

He muttered an anathema, faced about, and descended the steps. The beggar was still lounging at the corner of the street. Hamilton took out his handkerchief and blew his nose; and the beggar disappeared round the corner and was seen no more.

Hamilton walked on to Sixth Avenue, and stood there taking counsel with himself. As the result of his deliberations, he took a car down to Fourteenth Street, then across to Lexington Avenue, and so to a small house where he again rang at the door.

An elderly lady in a black dress and white cap and apron answered the ring.

"Is Miss Kitty Clive in?"

"I will see, sir. What name?"

"Captain Hamilton. I am a friend of Mr. Frank

Cunliffe, and would like to speak to her a moment
on business connected with him."   .

He handed out his card as he spoke, which had
engraved upon it his name and the branch of Her
Majesty's army to which he belonged. The lady
in black retired with it, leaving the visitor in the
hall. A due interval passed, and then Captain
Hamilton was told that he might step upstairs.

He found himself in a pleasant room, remark-
ably well ventilated, and containing, besides the
piano, a comfortable sofa that made one drowsy
to look at it, and chairs to match. He had hardly
had time to notice these things, when Miss Kitty
Clive entered.

As soon as Hamilton looked at her, he understood that he had to deal with a woman who was
without vanity, who was refined, who knew something of the world, and who possessed excellent
brains. She was not at all the ideal type of
opera singer. He was somewhat annoyed by this
discovery, for he had prepared himself for a much
more easily managed kind of person. She greeted
him with entire ease ; but there was a reserve in
her eyes to which her self-possessed manner only
lent emphasis. Hamilton, adopting his line on the
spur of the moment, decided to be simple and
straightforward.

"You are a relative of Mr. Cunliffe's, aren't
you ?" he said.

"Rather remote, Captain Hamilton ; remote
enough for friendship ! "

" I don't know if he ever spoke to you of me ? "
She moved her head in negation. " We got
acquainted at the club, you know, and have seen a
good deal of each other. What I wanted to say
was this : A common friend of ours, with whom I
dined last night, deputed me to invite Cunliffe to
join a sleighing party this morning to drive to his
home up at New Rochelle and take dinner. I
saw Cunliffe at the club later on, and gave him the
invitation, and he said he'd go. We were to meet
at the club this morning at ten o'clock. I was
there, but he didn't come. After a while one of the
fellows said he'd met him in the street, and that he
had told him he was going out of town."

At this point the Captain paused for breath, and
to think of what he should say next. Miss Clive
looked politely interested and said :

" What did you do ? "

" Well, I came here," the Captain replied, feeling
a trifle awkward. " I thought you might give me
an idea where he had gone."

" I'm afraid I can't," she returned, smiling.
" But I'll tell you where you might perhaps find
out."

" I shall be much obliged."

" You might ask at his lodgings."

" Ah—yes—well, the fact is, I went there first,
and they could tell me nothing. Then I recollected
his having spoken of you as his cousin, or something of that kind, and as I didn't know where else
to go—"

"I understand. I'm sorry I can't help you. It occurs to me, though—" She paused, and looked at the Captain with a very bright glance.

"Yes?" he said.

"I was thinking that perhaps he had mistaken about the sleigh-ride and was going to take the train up to New Rochelle."

"Oh, it couldn't be that, you know," said the Captain hastily.

"It was only an idea that struck me. You said you didn't know where he was going, except that he was going out of town ; and that seemed to me the most natural place, under the circumstances, for him to go."

"This woman is cleverer than she ought to be," said the Captain to himself. "I shouldn't wonder if she did know something about it after all." Aloud he said, "I'm afraid I've troubled you to no purpose."

"You have not troubled me at all. It is too bad of my cousin to have kept you waiting. Has the rest of the party started?"

"Well—that is, yes—they must have started some time ago. Ten o'clock, you know."

"Oh ! then how will you get there ? Will you go by train?"

"No ; it was the sleigh-ride we were going for," returned the Captain, beginning to wish that he had invented some more manageable story for the occasion. "The dinner without the sleigh-ride wouldn't be worth the trouble. I'll stay at home."

"You are English, are you not?" inquired Kitty.

"Yes, I'm a North-countryman. Why do you ask?"

"I have always wanted to go to England, and I like to see any one who comes from there. I hope to go some time."

"I hope you will. It's a nice place. You'll go to sing, I suppose?"

"That is my only chance. But there are so many better singers than I; I suppose I ought not to try it."

"I have heard your singing very well spoken of," said the Captain gallantly.

"But you have never heard the singing?" she said, laughing.

"Well, I'm only passing through here, you know, and a fellow doesn't get much time to himself—"

"Do you care for singing?"

"Indeed I do! I used to be able to hum a few bars myself."

"Would you like to hear me sing?"

"If you'd be good enough, there's nothing I'd like better."

"If you like it, you know, you can speak of it to your friends when you go back." She took her place at the piano, played meditatively for a few minutes, and then sang an English ballad. It carried the Captain back to a time now far in the distance, when he had heard that ballad sung in his own country—a time when he had his place in English society, and had looked forward to nothing less than to taking up with his present calling. He lost himself in these memories, and when the song ceased, he came to himself with a start, and with something like a sigh.

"But you are from the North," she said, before he could speak. "Then I suppose you know this :"—and she began to sing "Caller Herrin'."

When rendered by a fine contralto voice, such as Kitty undeniably possessed, this is one of the most wildly beautiful and rudely melodious songs in the language; you seem to see the fair-haired, blue-eyed, stately girl, the long gleaming sands and cold gray sea, and the shining fish borne aloft in the rustic wicker basket. The Captain listened in breathless delight. He could have listened forever. "Who'll buy my caller herrin'?" The rich voice rose and soared, and sank again. The Englishman's heart, surprised to find itself still in existence, after so many tough vicissitudes, acted in an irregular and turbulent manner. Where was he? on the coast of the North Sea? No, in New York, in a lodging house on Lexington Avenue, listening to an American girl sing. But he made this discovery only after she had stopped and, turning on her piano-stool, confronted him with her contagious smile.

"That's almost as good as going home again, Miss Clive," he said, after clearing his throat once or twice. " By Jove, though, it's worth coming to America to hear you sing it ! "

" Then you'll speak well of me to the people over there ? "

" Oh !—" said the Englishman ; and stopped. His cheeks and forehead reddened, and he bent his eyes on the floor. Had he actually been on the point of explaining to her why his recommen-dation would not have much weight just now in influential English circles? Was he about to reveal to her the history of his career, which was at least as checkered as that apocryphal one which passed current in the club, though not, perhaps, in all respects so reputable ? And all for a song ! no, no !

The Captain rose and walked over to the win-dow. There was a writing-table there, and upon it an open portfolio, with a blotting pad on one side. His glance fell upon it, and rested there unconsciously for a few moments. His thoughts were far away.

" I'm afraid I have been detaining you," said Kitty Clive.

" I don't know when to expect so much pleasure again," returned the Englishman, turning and extending his hand. " But I had no business to stay so long ; I'll say good-by now." He shook hands with her, and went out.

He reached the street, and, still preoccupied, had got nearly to the corner, when all at once he stopped as abruptly as if a chasm had opened before him in the pavement. Something hitherto latent in his mind had come to the surface with a shock that temporarily deprived him of the power of motion. So we see a face in the crowd, and do not know that we have seen it, until, an hour later perhaps, we realize it with a start, and all it implies.

It was a full minute before Captain Hamilton recollected himself sufficiently to notice that he was standing in a pool of half-frozen snow. He pulled himself together, and hurried on. If he had met Cunliffe at that moment, it is probable that he would have arrested him then and there, and taken him to the Central Office. But at all events he had completed the chain of evidence against him to his own satisfaction; and though Cunliffe might keep out of sight for a time he would be discovered sooner or later, and then—

"I hope that girl isn't in love with the fellow!" said the Captain to himself, "and yet she must be! She has been throwing me off the scent, and keeping me occupied, to give him time to get away! That's it, though I was too much off guard to see through it at the time. How she can sing! Well, I'd lay odds she doesn't suspect what he's up to, though he's been at it under her very nose! He's sharp enough to know that if he let her know his game she'd drop him like a shot! Well, just wait till I get hold of him, that's all! It's a shame that such a girl as she is should be wasting herself on such a blackguard!"

So thinking, the Captain took the Bowery cars in the direction of Bleecker Street.

CHAPTER XVI.

SUGGESTIONS.

CAPTAIN HAMILTON, for reasons satisfactory to those concerned, very seldom made his appearance at police headquarters ; and when he did so it was not in the character of an attaché of that institution, but as a gentleman at large, in quest of advice or assistance. His true standing was known to no one except Inspector Byrnes.

When he arrived there, accordingly, about one o'clock in the afternoon, he manifested a becoming unfamiliarity with the geography of the building, and required much guidance to find his way to the detective's sanctum. Once there, however, and the door closed upon him and his chief, this strangeness vanished like a cloud of steam in dry weather.

"Cunliffe has got off," were his first words.
" Went this morning."

"Have you made all inquiries?"

" Yes ; but he had two hours start." He went on to give a brief recapitulation of the events of the morning ; it was particularly brief as regarded his interview with Kitty Clive, for there were one or two reasons why the Captain felt indisposed to dilate upon all that he had seen or experienced at the abode of that young lady.   ˙

"There is no proof that he is out of the city," was the Inspector's comment.

"It is as good as proved that he is the man, though," rejoined the other; "and it looks as if he had made his pile and left."

"We can settle that, at any rate. Publish an advertisement that will call for an immediate answer. If it is answered promptly, we shall know that he is in the city and has not given up his business. If he doesn't answer it, we may conclude that he is either gone out of town because he is suspicious; or, if he is still here, does not intend to prosecute his scheme any further."

"He wrote the letters—I'm convinced of that," said Hamilton.

"Meanwhile," continued the Inspector, "we can make the usual investigation at the various points of departure as to whether a person answering his description has been seen. For my part, this move of his seems to me to tell rather in his favor. If he thought he was suspected, he must have perceived that running away would confirm the suspicion, and if he was guilty, but did not know he was suspected, there would be nothing to induce him to leave."

"A scared man does not always stop to reason," Hamilton said; "and if he does get away to Canada or to Europe, we couldn't get him back."

Scouts were sent to the various railway stations

and steamboat wharves, with the result that a man resembling Cunliffe was reported to have taken a ticket to Boston via the Shore Line Railway that morning. The description of the traveler was neither complete nor satisfactory ; but, assuming the identification to be correct, it indicated that he had probably gone to Canada. Meanwhile, an advertisement was put into the paper, and appeared the next morning.

That evening a telegram was received from Mr. Owens, announcing news. The Inspector and Hamilton, on arriving at his house, were shown a letter from the mysterious blackmailer that had just been received. It was an answer to the advertisement, and proved conclusively that if Cunliffe were the writer he must still be in New York.

After replying to the points presented in the advertisement, the letter had these words :

" It will be useless for you to attempt to discover who I am. My secret never can be revealed except by myself. I have means of knowing all that is being done to penetrate my concealment, and I adapt my measures accordingly. But unless you cease your efforts, I shall consider it an indication that the Lord has resolved to delay your punishment no longer. Be warned, and forbear !"

When Hamilton was first confronted by this reversal of his confident predictions, he was much crestfallen. But presently his demeanor changed, and he became very preoccupied and silent. He took no part in the discussion that ensued between

Mr. Owens and Inspector Byrnes, and when referred to for his opinion contented. himself with acceding to the suggestions which they had made. These suggestions did not embody any thing essentially novel in the mode of conducting the campaign, and there was a tacit feeling that the advantage so far remained with the unknown. But before the three separated Mr. Owens gave utterance to an idea that had not hitherto been broached.

"I am beginning to think," he said, "that this affair is not the work of a single man, but is a conspiracy concocted by a syndicate of men whose object is nothing less than Golding's ruin. Some of these men probably hold influential positions in the city, and, between them, are able to obtain information, more or less direct, of our every movement. If I am right, we have probably seen only the beginning of the difficulty. They are feeling their way ; but when they have become more familiar with the ground we may expect some gigantic operation, which will result in widespread ruin and panic. Golding is a powerful man, and in his downfall, if he fell, would be involved incalculable loss to public and private interests ; but a secret combination, defiant of moral principle, and willing to shrink at nothing, possesses boundless capacities for evil, and is much better able than any single rogue would be to defend itself against attack."

"I don't believe such a conspiracy could exist," returned the Inspector, promptly. "An association of men absolutely devoid of principle, and acting in direct defiance of the laws of the State, could not hold itself together. There could be no effective security against one or the other of them betraying the rest. The risks would be too great and the penalties would be too severe."

Owens shook his head doubtfully. " The temptations are also very strong," he observed. "As for the association together of unprincipled men, that has occurred before, and will again, and the secret has been kept, too—long enough, at least, to allow of a great deal of mischief being done. It is when the conspirators begin to quarrel over the plunder that the risk of detection becomes imminent ; but by that time the harm would be done, so far as we are concerned. Then you must consider how large the plunder in this case might be. Golding's actual property, vast as it is, is as nothing compared with the great interests and industries which he controls or manages. A band of able and well-informed men, knowing the ropes and having an inside track in affairs, could so manipulate things as to cause the profits of these industries to fall into their hands, and yet render it practically impossible to convict them of fraud. Besides, there undoubtedly exists a wide-spread business jealousy of Golding and animosity against him, and thousands of persons who had no knowledge of or part in the conspiracy would not be sorry to behold his downfall. Yes, Inspector, such a thing is possible ; and, assuming it to be a fact, we need not wonder that our efforts to identify the secretary of the association have been unsuccessful."

" How much has been netted so far by this blackmailer or syndicate of blackmailers ? " inquired Captain Hamilton.

" It is impossible to say at present. The sum may have been large or small, but more likely the latter than the former. As I said, they would only feel their way at first. Meanwhile, they could not disguise their true purposes better than by this pretense of ordinary blackmail."

" Mr. Owens," said the Inspector, after a pause, " you accused me the other day of being cynical. Perhaps I am ; but I don't think I was ever cynical on so large a scale as this. And yet you don't like to think ill of any one ! "

"Not of any one I know personally," replied Owens with a smile. " What I have just suggested is the result of my abstract meditations. I can cipher on a problem without reference to my private benevolence of character."

" It is a suggestion, sure enough," the Inspector returned, stroking his chin ; " but I must say you haven't convinced me. I still believe that if we can get our hands on the man who wrote those letters the whole business will come to a stop. And, even if you are right, that would still be the first step towards capturing the gang. If one of them is caught tripping, it will be my fault if we don't soon learn who the others are."

"How does my suggestion strike you, Mr. Hamilton?" Owens asked.

"I wouldn't like to form a conclusion upon it at once," that gentleman replied, "but, speaking off-hand, it doesn't seem to me improbable. A couple of brokers, two or three capitalists, and an out-sider or two, might make a very formidable com-bination, and a very difficult one to tackle. They could throw out many false scents, and complicate the matter in such a way as to bewilder any body. They might even get the actual criminal work done —the letters written—by some one who was igno-rant of their identity, and comprehended little or nothing of their designs. Thus, if that person were arrested, they would still be comparatively safe, and at all events would have time to take further measures to protect themselves."

"Whatever our opinions may be, they can be neither more nor less than guessing," the Inspector said, "and I don't see that they would practically help us much. If half the capitalists and brokers in Wall Street were in this supposed conspiracy against Mr. Golding, the fact would involve no essential change in our plan of operations. We shall gain nothing by allowing our attention to be distracted from the writer of the letters; until we have him, we can do nothing else. It makes no difference whether he is alone, or is acting for a syn-dicate, or is aware or not of the full bearing of his act; let us hunt him down to begin with, and then

we shall be in a much better position to handle the
rest of them—if any there are." ·

"Well, I agree with you there, Inspector," Owens
replied. "But we have already tried about every
device that can be thought of, and nothing has come
of it."

"We have inserted advertisements, and given
points, with a view to catching him in some of his
operations ; but the variations in the stocks have
not been large, and, as you say, his gains have
probably been small ; and there were so many
brokers on each side of the market that it has been
impossible to say which one of them all was acting
for our man. Suppose, now, that we go into the
thing on a bigger scale ?"

"In what way ?"

"Something like this. Have you a copy of the
cipher key ?"

"Here it is," said Owens ; and he took from his
pocket-book a slip of paper on which was written
the following :—

      "Bull, ... Up-town."
      "Bear, ... Down-town."
      "Western Union, ... Windsor."
      "Erie, ... Spoon."
      "Manhattan, ... Salvation."
      "Pacific Mail, ... Concord."
      "New York Central, . . . Berlin."
      "Lake Shore, ... Exchange."

And so on with a number of other stocks, the
proper designation of the stock being in each case

translated by some arbitrary word to be used as its representative.

"Now, what I propose is this," the Inspector continued, after glancing over the key. "Select some one of these stocks which is either well above par or well below it, and which there is every probability will remain where it is. If it is a low stock, advertise to the fellow to buy for all he is worth ; and if it is high, tell him to sell, and that you will bull or bear it, as the case may be, enough to make his fortune once for all."

"But that is the same principle we have been acting on already."

"The principle is the same, but the scale on which it is applied makes it different in effect. Suppose you take a stock at 50—one which nobody ever expects to go any higher. Forewarn your man that you are going to bull it. He will immediately order his brokers to buy all they can lay their hands on. Put a trained man on the floor to watch the bidding. It is ten to one that not more than two firms will be buying at that time ; and of those two the one who is taking in most, and doing it the most quietly, is the firm that our man is dealing with. When he has got as much as he can hold, jump in and send the thing ahead with all the means at your command, and high enough to make a sensation. Meanwhile, advertise him to sell out when it reaches a certain figure, as you will not be able to push it beyond that. Have your expert on hand when that figure is gained ; and the broker who sells largely then will, I venture to predict, be the same broker you spotted before ; but at any rate it is dollars to cents that he will be our man's broker. The transaction must be so managed that this sale will take place at a juncture when no one else will think of selling, but every body will be expecting the stock to go higher yet ; so that, no matter who may follow his example in unloading, he will be certain to lead the way."

"That certainly seems to be an improvement on any thing we have tried heretofore," Mr. Owens assented ; "but the stock market is such an uncertain thing, and any thing extraordinary is so apt to produce a panic, that the result may not be so clearly defined as would seem likely beforehand. It is worth considering, too, that, in case my hypothesis as to a conspiracy turns out to have some foundation, we should have half-a-dozen or more brokers following our 'tip' instead of only one. However, I think I know of a stock that will answer the purpose very well just at this time, and I will speak to Golding about it and get his opinion."

This ended the interview ; but after the Inspector and Hamilton had taken their departure the latter inquired whether, pending the consideration of the new scheme, he might be allowed to make another effort to pick up some information about Cunliffe.

"How now ? Have you got a new clew ?" smiled the Inspector.

"An expedient has occurred to me tnat I have not yet tried ; and as I let the man slip through my fingers I don't want to leave any stone un- turned to come up with him again."

"Do as you like," was the rejoinder ; "only keep me informed of your whereabouts, in case of any sudden need."

CHAPTER XVII.

ON THE ICE.

JOHN TALBOT, either because of his long legs, or in spite of them, was an excellent skater; and at the mature age of thirty or more he still retained a great deal of his early liking for the pastime. As a boy he had had enviable opportunities, living as he then did at the head of a long and broad valley, watered by a river with scarcely any current. In winter this river was in the habit of overflowing its banks (being assisted therein where necessary by dams judiciously applied); and when zero came hurrying down the valley on the wings of the north wind, and worked its will upon the sluggish stream for a night and a day, the fortunate youth of the neighborhood found themselves possessed in fee-simple of a domain of black ice, thirty miles in length by a mile in average breadth. Skates had no chance to get rusty in those days; and of all who used them John Talbot could go the fastest and cut the most surprising and sweeping circumbendibuses.

In comparison with so grand an arena, the narrow boundaries of the pond in Central Park were nothing less than comic ; but one gets accustomed to any thing, even to living for twenty years in a six by four stone dungeon, beneath low-water mark. Accordingly John had for several years past been in the custom of coming to the pond, once in a while, on winter evenings after business hours, and there, shod with gleaming steel, giving the city bumpkins an idea of how they cut up didos down east.

But during the winter of our story, his engagement to Miss Betty Claverhouse occurred, and gave him something even better than skating to think about. But the soul of man is an abyss which can never be filled ; and John Talbot, having made sure of Miss Betty Claverhouse, presently bethought himself whether he might not take in the Central Park pond likewise. Upon opening the subject to Betty, it appeared that skating was not among that admirable girl's accomplishments. But among her many virtues was a willingness to follow John's advice and adopt his suggestions in all things ; and when he represented to her the joys of the frosty science, and pictured the attractive appearance of the young ladies who practiced it, and furthermore dwelt upon the ridiculous ease and rapidity wherewith proficiency in it might be acquired—"Why," quoth John, " in comparison with type-writing, for instance, it is easier than falling off a hickory log ! "—when, I say, he had discoursed to her in this vein for a half hour or so, Betty was not only anxious to make her *début* upon the pond forthwith, but was well-nigh persuaded that she would be able to do the outward roll backwards, and to cut her initials, at the first attempt.

Thereupon, not to let the iron grow cool, John took the measure of her foot ; and on his way home the next afternoon he bought her as good a pair of skates as were to be had in New York City. Then, having eaten a hearty dinner together, and Betty having been fortified against the cold with plentiful wrappings, breast-plates, greaves, and gauntlets, the two young people embarked on a horse-car, and traveled up-town on their way to Central Park.

" Skating," said John, as they left the car at Fifty-ninth Street and proceeded on their way afoot, " is like falling in love. You are surprised, when you try it, to find how easy and agreeable it is."

" Falling in skating may be as easy," Betty replied (for she now began to feel vague apprehensions stiring within her feminine mind), " but I'm sure it can't be as agreeable. Dear me ! look there ! That poor girl was only just standing still, and all of a sudden she fell over backwards with an awful bump ! "

" She should not have stood still," said John calmly. " That is one of the most difficult feats to accomplish on the ice, and only the most skillful professors should venture to attempt it. That girl will know better another time. Thanks to her example, Betty, you know better already."

Partly reassured, Betty seated herself on a bench and allowed her betrothed to fasten on her skates. Then, sitting down beside her, he put on his own, " Now catch hold of my arm and stand up," said he.

" Goodness ! how tall they make one," murmured Betty, as she arose. " But what makes my ankles feel so loose ? Oh, John, I'm sure something's wrong !"

" You'll catch the idea directly." John replied. " Here we go ! " And putting his arm under her shoulders, he went forward a few paces, carrying rather than leading her with him. This brought them to the ice, and Talbot, giving a slight push with one foot, glided out upon the surface, Betty perforce accompanying.

So far all was well enough; but as Talbot swung round at the end of his slide, his companion, who was unprepared for such a maneuver, went all to pieces. The foot furthest from him followed his course ; the other foot continued on its direct course ; the consequence was that they crossed, tripping each other up, and somehow shooting upwards, Betty clutched her lover with a despairing grasp, one hand fastening upon his sleeve, the other upon the scarf which encircled his neck, causing the knot to tighten with such a jerk that John's eyes almost started out of his head. Involuntarily, and without a due regard to ultimate consequences, he strove to avert strangulation with his free hand. But fate, in the guise of Betty, was not to be denied. She achieved a wild evolution, in which all the members of her frame took part, though in disjointed and incongruous ways. This evolution was performed in a moment of time, and the most unimpassioned spectator would have found it impossible to analyze its component parts and place them in their due chronological order. As for John, who could scarcely be regarded as a spectator, and who, at that particular juncture, was certainly not unimpassioned, he was only conscious of an earthquake, accompanied by a cyclone, in the midst of which the whole surface of the frozen pond suddenly seemed to stand upright, dart behind him, and hit him a tremendous blow on the back of the head, while Betty rose in the air and, coming heavily in contact with him, knocked all the breath out of his body. That was the way it appeared to him ; but he was unquestionably the victim of a misapprehension. The simple explanation of the phenomena was that Betty had tripped him up and fallen on him. So far as his physical sensations were concerned, however, it might have happened either way indifferently. The reality was just as painful as the miracle would have been.

"Considering how short a time we have practiced together, Betty, we did that very well," faltered John, as he began to realize that the afterpart of his skull had not expanded to the dimensions of the prize pumpkin with which his father had taken the medal at the cattle-show eighteen years previous. "Are you hurt ? "

" No—John—I think not," she gasped in reply.

"But oh! this is dreadful! Something seemed to catch my heels and pull them up into the air. I'm sure you are mistaken in thinking me a good skater."

"No," returned John, still faintly, as he extracted Miss Claverhouse from amongst his ribs and assumed a sitting posture; "no, Betty, I am never mistaken. The trouble was that I got in your way. You would have done it much better alone."

"Oh, I don't want to do it all!" the lady exclaimed, in a tone that carried assurance of her sincerity. "Besides, I heard something crack as we went down, and I'm sure we shall tumble in."

"Don't be alarmed, Betty; it was only my head that cracked, not the ice; and my head is too full of brains to admit of your getting into it. It is my heart that is your home, you know. But really, now, don't you want to take just one more turn? See how pleased the people are with us already!"

"Truly, John, I would much rather not. But if you want to I'll sit down and wait till you have finished."

"Well, no; I don't believe I care so much about skating as I thought I did," replied John, with the air of a cloyed voluptuary. "I don't remember remarking it before, but it is a great drawback having the ice hard, instead of soft, like a feather mattress. Let's see; do you think you could skate to the bank?"

"If you pulled me I think I could get there sitting."

"Perhaps that would be best. It is a new figure in skating, though not so exciting as our first one. Here goes, then; but try to look as if you were accustomed to it."

With this admonition John climbed wearily to his feet, and laying hold of Betty by the tail of her jacket, he drew her gently to the shore. No casualty attended this performance; and Betty schooled her features into an expression of strained placidity which added greatly to the picturesque effect.

The skates were removed. John gave Betty his arm, and they started homewards. "After all," he said, "perhaps you had better not give up type-writing for the career of a professional skater. The competition is almost as great; and, taking one thing with another, I'm not sure that you don't appear to as good advantage at the type-writer as on the ice."

"I shouldn't mind about that, John, dear, if you were pleased with me; but I agree with you that type-writing suits me best. Besides, I can do that without your help. By the way, what made you send that man to me?"

"Send you a man, Miss Claverhouse! What man?"

"Mr. Hamill, you know. I couldn't do it at home, because I have no machine there; and I'm kept busy all the time at the office."

" Pray, my dear, what does Mr. Hamill want you to do for him ? And in the first place, who the devil is Mr. Hamill ? "

" Oh, John.!—why, I only know him from you. If you didn't want me to know him, why did you send him to me ? "

John was silent a moment, and then asked, " What sort of a looking man was Mr. Hamill ? "

" Oh, I think he looks nice enough, don't you ? . He talks like an Englishman, and has side whiskers too. But of course there are plenty of people who can do his copying easier than I could."

" He wanted some copying done, did he ? "

" Why, John, how funny you are ! He said you told him I could. You must have been thinking of something else when you were talking to him."

" I guess I must have been. Did he ask you any thing about me ? or about Mr. Cowran ? or about yourself ? "

" No : I think Mr. Cunliffe was the only one he spoke of."

" Yes ; and what did he say about Cunliffe ? "

" Let me see ! He asked whether you had heard from him since he went away."

" What did you tell him ? "

" I said that I only knew of one letter, written when he got to Boston and had just seen that man. You know."

" I know. Well ? "

" Well, we talked about that a few minutes ; and then he asked whether he was going to stay in Boston, and—oh, I don't know ! There was nothing of any consequence. But what made you think I could do any work for him ? "

" It is a peculiarity of mine that I sometimes say one thing when I think I am saying just the opposite. It is called heterophemy, and is characteristic of many great men. Is Mr. Hamill going to call again ? "

" No, I suppose not. He said he was sorry that he couldn't engage me ; and by the way, I forgot? "

" What did you forget ? "

" Why, he asked me not to say any thing to you about it, because it might hurt your feelings. But I didn't see why it should hurt your feelings, so I didn't remember not to."

" I'll forgive you ! " said John. But he was very taciturn the rest of the way home.

CHAPTER XVIII.

CUNLIFFE'S BENEFACTOR.

INASMUCH as Miss Claverhouse has spoken of a letter written by Frank Cunliffe to his friend John Talbot, it would seem scarcely courteous to withhold the letter from the reader, especially as it may serve to enlighten a situation which has already become somewhat obscure.

The letter was a long one, and was dated at Boston, a couple of days after Cunliffe's mysterious disappearance. After touching upon a few unimportant matters, it continued as follows :—

"But I have not yet told you the occasion of my abrupt departure. Three nights ago, when I got home rather late from the club, I found a letter on my table with the Boston post-mark. The handwriting was unfamiliar to me ; and I should have suspected it of being a dunning application, only that, so far as I could remember, I had never bought any thing in Boston that I had not paid for, if, indeed, I ever bought any thing there besides a cigar, a pair of gloves, or a ticket to the theater. I was tired, however, and thought I wouldn't open the letter until the next morning. But when I got undressed, and was sitting before the fire in my dressing gown, I lighted a cigarette, and then I thought I might as well have a look at that letter. So I opened it ; and looked first at the signature.

" Did I ever happen to speak to you of Fowler Morgan ? probably not, for I had almost forgotten him myself.   I knew him when I was in college, which is now a good many years since.   He was considerably older than I, and was in the law-school when I entered the Freshman class.   He took a fancy to me for some reason—I forget what —and we were a great deal together.   I both liked him and disliked him.   I knew him to be an un-principled man ; but there was a fascination about him : there was something undeveloped in me that sympathized with something developed in him. He would come into my room and talk to me by the hour, telling me all sorts of things about him-self and his experiences, and what he meant to do in the world : I listened to it all, though there was a great deal that I had better not have listened to. I felt that he was inoculating me with low views of life—views which I disapproved of ; and yet I liked him to come, and preferred his company to any one else's.

" His mother had saved up money enough to send him to the law-school ; but he admitted to me that he was studying the law only in order to be able with more safety to evade or defy it.   He used to say that society was a humbug, and that every body would be a thief if he knew how to be without getting punished.   ' I'm just like all the rest of them,' he said, ' except that I'm not afraid. I don't want any sentiment or religion or nice sense of honor in mine. I'm going to get money and have a good time ; and I'm not going to starve myself to death either ! '

" ' You're a nice boy,' he often used to say to me, ' but you haven't got the stuff in you : you're handicapped with all that nonsense about respectability and honesty and so on. You'll never make a living for yourself ; if somebody doesn't give you money you'll never have any. They say God helps those who help themselves. I say, the devil helps those who won't help themselves. I'll tell you what I'll do with you, Frank. When I die—and I don't expect to live to a hundred—I'll leave you my money. I will as sure as I'm sitting here. You'll have forgotten all about it by that time ; but it may come in handy just the same.'

" Of course, I thought nothing of that, and forgot about it, as he had said I would, very soon after he left the college. I have never known, from that day to this, what he did with himself. At intervals—rather long ones—I used to run across him ; he always greeted me on the same footing as of old ; but his proceedings were evidently not of the kind that seek the light, and he has occasionally warned me not to call him by his real name. I fancy he was in jail at one time, though I don't know what for. As you may imagine, I was not exactly proud of my acquaintance with him, though still I always felt that old unregenerate lik-

ing for him. Later, I believe he got into politics, under some other name ; and I presume that
is where he made his money.

"I also have reason to think that he was married
at one time, but he never spoke to me of having a
wife, and probably they did not live together. Afterwards he drifted out of my field of vision altogether, and I have not seen him for a number of
years—I don't know exactly how many. I have
always suspected him of being a thorough-paced
rogue ; but I have always been careful not to seek
confirmation of this suspicion ; and several times,
when he has seemed to be on the point of telling
me some episode of his career, I have stopped him,
and said that I preferred to know nothing about it.

"Well, that was the state of affairs as between
him and me when I opened the letter the other
night. The name signed at the end of it was
Fowler Morgan.

"I read the letter with a good deal of interest ;
and my interest increased as I went on. It was
a queer document, rambling and rather inco-
herent at first, but presently I gathered that the
man was ill and expected to die. This statement
was accompanied with a good deal of sacrilegious
allusion, characteristic of him, but unusually revolting in such a connection. He went on to say that
he was alone in the world, and had no one but his
lawyer and doctor to look after him. ' I want to
see you, Frank, before I peg out,' the letter continued, ' and I don't want you to lose a minute in com-

ing here, either. We were always pals, in a sort of way, and I could have made a man of you, if you had had more sense ; but, any way, you were about the only man I took a real shine to ; and I'll prove it, too, before I'm done with you. But you needn't think I'm such a fool as to suppose that you would travel two hundred miles at this time of the year to see a pal who is dying and has no one to say a good word to him. Oh, no, I know a trick worth two of that ! You come here, Frank, and you'll find it the most paying investment you ever made. It's a straight tip I'm giving you, my boy. Do you remember a promise I made to you when we were in the college together ? I do if you don't : and I can keep a promise, when I want to, as well as another man. Come down here by the next train, my boy, and give me a chance to show that I'm a man of my word ! '

"I read the letter over, and smoked another cigarette ; and by the time I had finished that I had made up my mind to go to Boston the next day. I had more than one reason for being willing to go. Things have occurred lately that have made me uneasy and nervous, and a change of scene would be a relief. Whether it was a fancy of mine or not, I have had an impression of late that I was being dogged by detectives ; and this seemed a good opportunity to give them the slip. Then there was the wish (stronger than you might suppose, or than I myself should have considered likely beforehand) to stand by Morgan in his last hours ; and finally, I am free to confess that his hint as to a legacy had no small influence with me. I have been hard up lately, and at my wits' end to know what to do. This seemed a solution ; at all events I went ; and in order not to be annoyed by my detectives (real or imaginary) I was at the pains to get up at half-past five the next morning and leave the house an hour later, after having given the housemaid five dollars to admit no inquisitive persons to my rooms, should any call, and to answer no questions should any be asked.

" I got my breakfast at a restaurant on Sixth Avenue (feeling a good deal like a defaulting bank cashier on his way to Canada, except that I had no stolen funds in my possession), read the papers, smoked a cigar, and then set out for the railway station ; and, as luck would have it, I met a fellow I knew on the corner of Forty-second Street. However, I got off all safe, and arrived here in due course. After getting a room at the hotel, I had some dinner, and then went to the address given in Morgan's letter.

" It was a commonplace, respectable-looking house near the outer confines of Tremont Street. I was admitted at once on giving my name, and found the interior as featureless and barren as the outside. Every thing was orderly and conventional, but entirely without character or individuality ; no doubt an upholsterer had been given a certain sum of money and ordered to ' furnish up to it ' according to his own taste. This interior gave me a new impression of the essential empti-

ness and barrenness of Morgan's mind. His brain
was always busy plotting and contriving, but he
had no resources, no character, no moral or intellectual substance out of which to make any thing.
He might be the occasion of a lot of mischief, but
he was nothing but a sort of phantom, after all.

"I was taken up to his bed-room, and there he
was lying in the bed, with his night-dress on, and a
servant, or hired nurse, to attend to him and give
him his medicine. He was as pale as a corpse
already, and as thin as a mummy ; but his face was
newly shaven, his hair oiled and brushed, and his
mustache waxed. He used to be a handsome fellow, and was always a dandy in his personal appearance. He kept that instinct up still.

"He gave me a lean, cold hand, and grinned,
showing his white teeth, and wrinkling the skin
about his mouth and eyes. His voice was very low,
but it had the same jaunty tone as ever, and his
conversation was as plentifully sprinkled with pro-
fanity. If he had ever committed wickedness in his
life (as there can be no doubt he had), it was evident that he felt not the slightest remorse, and only
so much comprehension of what remorse meant as
to be anxious to show none. Did you ever see a
death-bed repentance ? They may be edifying ;
but this spectacle made me realize as vividly as any
thing what an ugly and horrible thing it must be to
live and die without ever having cared to do or to
be any thing good or useful.

"'I know what you came for, Frank,' he said at

last. 'You came for money, d—— you! don't deny it. Well, I'm going to hell, and have no more use for mine, so you can have it. Much good may it do you, my boy! May you keep drunk for twelve months and commit all the crimes in the calendar! But you'll never have as good a time as I've had! I've beaten every thing and every body that I've had any thing to do with. Oh, I've been a devil: nobody ever touched me that didn't regret it! It's just as I told you when we started out— society is a set of frauds and cowards, and the only men who get any solid satisfaction out of life are the men of my sort! Look at me now!'

"I did look at him; and he must have seen something in my face that told him what I was thinking of. It seemed to put him out a little; the swagger that he immediately assumed had something appealing and pathetic in it.

"'I'm all right!' he said. 'What if I am rotting in my coffin by this time to-morrow? I've had my fling, haven't I? No one has got ahead of me, has there? Is there any man or woman, living or dead, can say that they ever found a soft place in Fowler Morgan? Do you suppose that doesn't make me feel good? You don't know me! They can come and spit at me when I'm dead, G—d d——n 'em! but that isn't now. The only thing I'm sorry for is that my dying won't——'

"However, I don't know why I should repeat all the ravings this poor devil indulged in; it was bad enough to hear them once for all. Meanwhile

he was dying fast, and he knew it ; and what was
more, he was really in ghastly terror of the end,
and was talking to try and keep up his courage.
His voice grew so low that I could scarcely hear it.
At ten o'clock that evening the doctor came in—a
fine, ruddy, powerful-looking fellow—and examined
him.   The disease was some affection of the vis-
cera, and was now in its last stages.   Morgan kept
his eyes on the doctor with an odd expression, as.
if he would have liked to drink his blood and so
get the health and strength that were so conspicuous in him ; and though he seemed to hate him
for being so well and hearty, yet he found a sort of
comfort in having him near ; and at last he said,
'Say, doc, what will you take to stay here until
to-morrow ?'   The doctor said he couldn't do it.
'Come, now,' said Morgan, 'take a thousand dollars and stay ! I'll give you cash.'   The doctor
shook his head.   Morgan went on raising his bid
until he had offered him ten thousand dollars to
spend the night in that room.   Then the doctor
looked him in the face and said, 'I'd stay for nothing if it would do you any good.   But it would
not, and I have other patients to look after ; I want
my regular fee, and no more.'   Morgan said, 'If
you don't stay, G—d d——n your soul, you shall
have nothing !   Now, then !   Ten thousand dollars
or nothing !   And with that he dragged out a wallet
from under the pillow, and actually took out of it
ten one thousand dollar bills, and shook them at
the doctor, and whispered —he could not speak

aloud—'There you are! Ten thousand—or nothing!' The doctor just turned to the nurse and gave some directions about the medicine, and then moved towards the door. I expected to see Morgan fly into a fury of rage; but instead of that he quieted right down and said: 'Say, doc, how am I getting on? how long do you give me?' The doctor faced about on him and said: 'Do you want to know the truth?' 'Yes, if you know how to tell it.' The doctor waited a moment or two, as if doubting whether to take him at his word or not; at last he replied, 'You can't live longer than till noon to-morrow.' Then he went out.

"Morgan glanced at me with a terrible expression; but the next instant he forced one of his grins and said: "There goes a liar and a fool. He thought he'd scare me, but I'm more of a man than he is, now! As for the money, it'll go into your pocket instead of his, that's all.' He stuffed the bills back in his wallet, and then lay for a long time—an hour at least—without uttering a word. I can only imagine what his thoughts were during that time. I would not have liked to have had them. Finally he roused himself and stared round the room, ending at last on me. He had changed; his nerve was leaving him; every little while he gave a shiver, and glanced about as if something frightened him. 'That's right, Frank,' he said to me; 'you won't go back on me, will you? I'll make it right with you, never fear! This is my bad time; I'll be all right—again in the morning.' He kept shivering more and more, and his face grew even more haggard. It was hideous to see those carefully waxed mustaches on such a face. By and by he got hold of his wallet again, and took a key out of it, and told me to unlock a desk near the bed, and bring him what I found in it. There were two wills, dated the same day, and, as I saw when he opened them, signed and attested. He put his hand on one of them and whispered, ' This gives it to you. If you hadn't come, I'd have burned it and kept the other.' He lay there holding one of the wills in one hand and the other in the other ; and so he lay, shivering and glaring, and now and then making odd little noises in his throat—thin, falsetto sounds—until nearly four in the morning.

" I was not in the least sleepy, but I have never passed such disagreeable hours as those were. I wanted to go away—I'd have given all the little I'm worth to have done it—but I couldn't. I felt that so long as he was human I must stay with him. At four o'clock he sat up in bed, and I thought something ugly was going to happen. But he said he wanted to be moved over to the fire.

" There was a big open grate, with a heaped up, glowing coal fire in it. At one side of it was a sofa for the nurse to sleep on. It was his idea to be lifted on to that. We took him up and laid him there, and pulled round the sofa so that it stood in front of the fire, for he seemed unable to get warm enough. There he lay, with a will in either hand ; and when he found himself settled to his satisfaction he turned to me with a cunning leer and said, 'Now I've got you. If you stir out of this room, I'll put your will on the fire. If you stay till the doctor comes in the morning, I'll burn the other.' I said nothing ; the whole situation made me feel sick. ' Do you know who the other is in favor of ? ' he asked. ' It's in favor of the man I hate most in the world ! ' he said.

"So there I sat and waited—for what, was more than I could tell. It seemed like a sort of race between death, Morgan, and myself. Death was sure to catch him before long ; but Morgan lay ready to do the most harm he could to the only man in the world who could be called his friend, if that man should turn aside before the race was over. As for me, as I sat there I conceived such a loathing of this money of Morgan's, and of the idea that I was going to inherit it, and such a disgust at this sordid suspense, that more than once I was on the point of jumping up and throwing the wretched will into the fire myself, or leaving the room in order that he might do so. But I abstained, not, as I honestly think, from any base motive, but because after all the man was dying, and he wished me to be there. He was treating me as if I were the lowest kind of sneak and blackguard ; and yet he considered me, I suppose, as good a man as had ever lived in the world, and cared for me as much as such a man as he was capable of caring for any body. It was a strange

" he
and revolting position ; and I shall never ·ed
get it.

" During the last hours of darkness not a syllable
was uttered by any body ; I sat most of the time·
looking at the fire ; but I was conscious of Morgan's eye fixed upon me, watching me as a cat
watches a mouse, or rather as one man watches
another whom he suspects of an intention to murder him. I felt, and perhaps he did, that the
strain was wearing on him, and would probably
shorten the few hours he had to live ; indeed, he
weakened and sank visibly ; but he held on with a
forlorn, ghastly pertinacity ; there was nothing else
for him in the world.

" At last the light of dawn shone through the
crevices of the blinds into the gas-lit room ; and I
could hear the wind rising and sweeping down the
street, pure and freezing, making me loathe still
more the hot, close air of the bedchamber. Sounds
began to be audible from without : people hurrying
along, and a horse-car jingling by. Another change
came over Morgan, and it came suddenly ; he
seemed to sink all at once into a heap ; his head
fell forward on his breast, and he breathed short
and sharply, trying to moisten his lips with his
tongue ; his eyes rolled this way and that in a kind
of speechless terror and despair. I held a glass of
water to his mouth, and he tried to drink some,
but could not.

" The door-bell rang downstairs. The sound
went through Morgan's body like a galvanic shock.

hand :

satisfied up, gasping for breath, and stretching
ar neck towards the door. Steps were coming upstairs ; the door opened, and there was the doctor.

" Morgan gave a cry ; whether it signified triumph,
or rage, or whether it was an involuntary shriek of
exhausted strength, I don't know. He twisted
himself round toward the fire, and swayed over,
with the will in his hand, as if to put it on the coals.
I sprang to save him, but I was not in time. He
fell over into the grate, with his face against the
red-hot coals, and had lain so for a second or more
before the doctor and I could pull him off. We
laid him on his back on the sofa. His face was
already unrecognizable—hideously disfigured. I
think that he lived for a few minutes after, but I am
not sure ; it may have been simply an involuntary
quivering of the nerves.

" Meanwhile, the will that he had put on the
fire had burned up, without either of us attending
to it. But when Morgan was quite dead, the doctor picked up the other will, which lay on the floor
beside the fender, and, after glancing at it, said
rather drily, ' I may congratulate you, General
Weymouth. That is your name, I suppose ?'

" I didn't understand him. ' My name is Cunliffe,' I said.

" ' I beg your pardon ! This will devises the
property to General Weymouth, and I presumed, as
he burned the other, that you must be the heir. I
know the burned will was in favor of a Mr. Cunliffe, for I witnessed the signature. I hope the

poor creature made no mistake at the last," he added, giving me a sudden glance, 'and destroyed the one he meant to save.'

" It was a moment before I comprehended what had happened ; but when I did, a load went off my soul and left me feeling all over new ; such a burst of joy I never experienced ; and I knew what it meant to thank God. As soon as I could speak, I said, ' There was no mistake, doctor. Mr. Morgan did just as I wished him to do.'

"' Ah ! ' he said, with another keen look. ' Well ; if you are content, no one else has a right to complain. But all this is rather irregular. We must get a lawyer or somebody to take the proper measures here. If you consent, I will send one of the servants ; ' he rang the bell, and the servant was despatched on his errand. The doctor and the nurse busied themselves with the body, and I opened the window blinds and stood looking out.

" Thank God it fell out as it did. But it is an interesting speculation whether Morgan burned the will he meant to ; and, if not, whether he realized before he died that he had enriched the man he called his worst enemy ! "

CHAPTER XIX.

IN DOUBT.

SUCH was the substance of the letter written by
Cunliffe to John Talbot, who communicated
something of its general purport to the mistress of
his heart, Miss Betty Claverhouse. Betty, in turn
had given certain echoes of it to that interesting
stranger, Mr. Hamill, and Mr. Hamill, acting upon
the hints thus obtained, started for Boston, and
arrived there an hour after Cunliffe, having attended Morgan's funeral, had left Boston on his
way back to New York. The events of his sojourn
there had made a profound impression on him.

His first act upon reaching the city was to call
on Kitty Clive. He told her the story of his experience, and she had no difficulty in recognizing
in Fowler Morgan the Fowler whom General Weymouth had mentioned to her in the narrative of
his own life. It was apparent, therefore, that Morgan had at least contemplated an act of restitution ; and either accident, or possibly some incalculable caprice of the mind at the very moment of
dissolution, had carried the remote contingency
into actual effect. General Weymouth would be
a couple of hundred thousand dollars the richer ;

"but," said Cunliffe, turning a grave look upon Kitty, after she had enlightened him as to the general's relations with Morgan, "I have had a lesson which is worth a great deal more than that to me."

"I am glad of that," she replied; "and I am glad that the general is to get restitution at last; but for all that I wish you could have had at least half of the money."

"Such money could have brought me no good," he replied. "The only money worth having is what a man honestly earns—or, at the least, honestly inherits—for himself. If I had taken Morgan's money, I should have made myself a party to his rascality. If the temptation had been offered me, I hope I should have been man enough to resist it; but I am glad I was not given the opportunity."

"But if you had not known that the money was fraudulently come by—and it is only the accident of my acquaintance with the general that gave you the knowledge—then, surely, there would have been no reason to refuse."

"It may sound Quixotic in me if I say that I would refuse," answered Cunliffe, "and I am not speaking of the abstract rights of the question, but only as it affects myself. If you had seen what I have seen during these last few days you would think as I do. I have always felt that there was a great deal in me that was like Morgan, and that, if our circumstances had been reversed, I might have

become very much as he was. But even as it is, if
I have done no active and malicious mischief, I
have done no good. I have had no aim but to be
as idle and comfortable as I could. I have spent
all my income on myself, and when I lost it,
instead of setting to work to get some honest employment, I only sat down and wished that something would turn up to relieve me. Now that I
look back upon it I can see that I was not very far
from becoming a criminal then, and if Morgan had
come to me at that time, and proposed some shady
transaction or other, that was not too openly and
brazenly flagitious, I believe I should have been in
great danger of striking hands with him. And if I
had once begun, I know enough of myself to know
that I would not have stopped this side of State
prison."

" You know yourself very little to think such a
thing," returned Kitty, the color coming slowly
into her face.

" You have never felt criminal impulses, and you
can not judge of them. I have felt, for some weeks
past, a sensation as if, somehow, crime were not
far off from me, and that notion about which I
spoke to you, that I was being dogged by detectives, was probably connected with it."

Kitty moved her head as if about to speak, but
on second thought seemed to alter her purpose.
She kept regarding Cunliffe with a troubled look.

" Such a man as I am can not afford to run any
risks with his moral character," he went on, " and

I have made up my mind to strike out a new path
while the influence of this experience is still fresh
upon me. I have sent in my resignation to the
club, and to-morrow I am going to look for something to do. And I will find something, too, if it's
only to be janitor to an apartment-house."

"I do not say you ought to do nothing," Kitty
observed in an abstracted tone. "I dare say that
some business that is suited to you would make
you happy, no matter whether you actually needed
the money it brought you or not. But that is no
reason why you should refuse money that you had
not earned if it came to you. Suppose, for instance,
that Maxwell Golding could be compelled to restore
you the money you lost in his stocks—wouldn't
you feel that you had a right to that?"

"I don't want any thing from Maxwell Golding
or any body else," returned Cunliffe with a smile.
"I lost my money gambling, and Golding, even if
he had known that my money was among his win-
nings, had a perfect right to keep it. Besides,
Kitty, it isn't money that I most care for—though
I shouldn't blame you for thinking otherwise. In
fact, it is a good while since I began to care most
for something else; and yet, if this affair had not
occurred, I doubt if I should have had the courage
and self-respect to acknowledge it to myself—or to
speak of it to you."

Something in the tone of his voice seemed to
startle Kitty, and an expression of mingled incredulity and fear came into her face. As his eyes

met hers she put out one hand as if to ward off a blow.

"You must hear it, Kitty," he said, "for this is the time to tell you. I love you." He stood up before her and said again, "I love you, Kitty—I am all yours, heart and soul. Don't say you can't —you have not tried—do try to love me! to have you my wife!—Kitty, if there is any thing a man may do to win you let me know it!—I can not hear you say no! I love you—you are heaven and earth to me—you are the only want and passion of my heart! Say that I spoke too soon, or that you haven't thought of it—that you must have time, but don't tell me that you can never love me!"

She leaned back in her chair and pressed her hands over her eyes. "Oh, Frank, Frank!" she said.

"It need not be now; only let it be to come," he went on. "I told you now because this is the beginning of a new life. I am going to begin to be a man; I only want you to let me feel that, if I succeed, I may hope to have you; whatever I became would be worthless without you. Just the hope is all I ask. Can it not be? It must be!"

"I am afraid! I am afraid!" she murmured, still covering her face. "I can't—I can never tell you!"

"What can you not tell me?" he said, kneeling on one knee beside her, and trying to draw away her hands. "You need not say—you needn't decide this moment whether you care for me. I

didn't expect it, love ; how could I ? Only say you
may—say you will try ! I will not ask you to be
my wife until I can support you, Kitty, and that
may be a long while yet."

"Don't touch me !" said she in a low but
vehement tone. "Let me alone—let me think !
I don't know what to do."

Cunliffe rose and drew back a step, trying to
fathom what might be passing in the girl's mind.
He was himself in somewhat of a tremor from the
strength of the emotion which he had expressed,
and which, in its overmastering sway, was a revelation even to him. We do not know our souls
until we strip off the fetters of habit and lethargy
that bind them. Cunliffe could see that Kitty was
under the influence of some passionate feeling, but
of what nature it was beyond him to determine.
That he had awakened it seemed evident ; but
whether or not he was the subject of it was another
question.

After a minute or two Kitty got up from her
chair and paced twice or thrice up and down the
room. At length she came up to Cunliffe and took
both his hands in hers.

"Frank, we must both wait before committing
ourselves," said she. "I expected nothing so little
as this ; I have never imagined you would look on
me as any thing but a friend—a friend and cousin.
As long as I was only that, it did not make much
difference what else I was, or what I did. But to
be the only woman in the world to you—that would

change every thing; it would involve your knowing things that I never meant or wanted you to know. I can only now say that if I had foreseen what was to come I should have acted differently in several ways. I · must take counsel with myself, and decide whether—this—is possible. I want you to be happy, Frank," she added, with a faltering of the voice, " but I don't want you—or either of us—to make a mistake that could never be rectified. Let every thing be as if you had never spoken, for a few days; then come again, if you still think it best, and I will talk openly with you. I can say nothing more now, or I would say too much."

" I have perfect trust in you, Kitty," said Cunliffe, trying to kiss her hands, which she would not allow. " Nothing can alter the love I feel for you, except to increase it. If you have been drawn into any other engagement—" She shook her head——" well, then, there can be nothing else to separate us; I mean, if you can love me."

She made no reply, but drew her hands from his, and turned her face away from him. He went to the door.

" I shan't stay away long," said he ; " my thoughts will never be away from you at all. I care for nothing but to be with you always."

" It shall not be long," she answered, without looking at him ; " but, until then, good-by!"

After leaving her, Cunliffe walked along the streets in a state of preoccupation so profound that

he did not know where he was going. At last he
came to himself ; and finding, by consulting his
watch, that it was late enough for Talbot to have
returned home from his office, and his wanderings
having brought him into the neighborhood of the
house, he repaired thither and found his friend
in.

"Hullo, Cunliffe, I'm glad you came out alive,"
was the latter's greeting. "You look like your
letter, and I couldn't say any worse of you."

"I feel as if I had been away about twenty
years," said the other. "Has New York changed
much since I was here ? "

"It is no better. By the way, did you happen to
run across any of your New York acquaintances
while you were there ? "

"No."

"You know a man named Hamilton, don't
you ? "

"Captain Hamilton—an Englishman—visiting at
the club. Yes."

"Well, I have reason to think that he is not all
that he appears to be ; and when you next meet
him I wouldn't confide to him your bosom secrets,
if I were you. He might give you away."

"What gives you that idea ? "

"Oh, a little bird told me. He was looking after
you the other day, and when he learned (by an
inadvertence of my own, for which I have been
kicking myself ever since) that you were gone to
Boston he left for that town in such a hurry that

he forgot to take the last syllable of his name with him."

"Are you in earnest ? What is the meaning of it ? "

" I am in earnest ; but you ought to know better than I what your sins have been. Don't confess them to me, though ; for in case I am called as a witness I want to be able to say ' I don't know,' with a clear conscience."

" Hamilton, of all men ? " muttered Cunliffe, in deep perplexity. " I knew something was going on behind the scenes ; but how comes Hamilton to be mixed up in it? And what can it be, anyway ?"

Meanwhile the following telegrams had passed between Boston and the Detective Bureau in New York. The first was from Boston :

"C. has left here. He attended funeral of No. 2007. Suspicious circumstances. Wire instructions." To this came the answer :

" C. certainly not our man. Letter answering personal posted, and received here during his absence. Return at once."

And Captain Hamilton took the next train to New York.

CHAPTER XX.

PANIC.

CAPTAIN HAMILTON had a quality which, as much perhaps as any other, has been conducive to human knowledge and the progress of enlightenment—the quality of curiosity. He liked to inform himself as to what other people were doing, and whenever possible to see with his own eyes what was going on. A city like New York affords an almost inexhaustible field of observation to the intelligent foreigner ; and among the many spectacles worth looking at, perhaps none yields in interest to that of Wall Street when speculation is sharp, and quotations are running up and down like the waves of a stormy sea.

One morning, shortly after the events above narrated, the Captain found himself on the lower part of Broadway ; and, as luck would have it, he suddenly saw the broad back of Gilbert Cowran a few paces in front of him on the sidewalk. He quickened his steps and overtook him.

"Oh, Hamilton," said the lawyer, "you are just in time to see some fun. Have you half an hour at liberty ? "

"Always at your service for at least so long," the other replied cheerfully. "What is going on to-day?"

"They say that some of the big fellows are out on a foraging expedition. Come along and we'll have a look at them!"

"I should like it of all things," said the captain. "I've been on the Bourse two or three times, and once I saw a young fellow walk quietly out and stand at the top of the steps, and take a revolver out of his pocket and blow the top of his head off. But I understand that it is much more exciting here."

"We don't blow the tops of our heads off, as a rule," Cowran answered, "but we have plenty of calisthenics, and we exercise our lungs. Americans are not tragic, as a nation—not even dramatic; they believe that a man isn't necessarily beaten because he's knocked down once or twice; they are always ready to try again, and to help others to do so. But they have tremendous larks, all the same, and sometimes, to tell the truth, the fun gets pretty serious. I know that of my own knowledge."

"I recollect," said the Captain, smiling. "That time you and Golding had a little bout."

"As to that matter," remarked Cowran, after a moment's hesitation, "I feel bound to modify some of the language that I used in your hearing the other day. I was very bitter against Golding at the time I was cleaned out, because I believed that he had done it of malice aforethought, to get me out of the way; and I have borne a grudge against him for it ever since, and haven't spared to give my opinion of him in season and out. But I am convinced, now, that I did him injustice. He did not know that I was in the market at the time, and he had not foreseen the contingency that obliged him to reverse all his plans at a moment's notice. What he had said to me previously had been said in good faith. When the affair was over, and I was beggared, I went to him and spoke my mind without hunting for polite phrases; and he made no reply whatever; but when I had finished, he turned in his chair and went on writing. That put me in a greater rage than ever; but I can understand now that I interpreted his silence the wrong way. He had a pride of his own, and when I attacked him without waiting to ask him how it happened he was not going to trouble himself to make any explanations. I took it for granted that he did all he could to keep me down afterwards; but he is a bigger man than I gave him credit for being, and really seems to be above personal animosities. I have lately discovered that, so far from trying to keep me down, he was the means of putting within my reach the means of getting up again. He did it, and he took pains not to let me know that he was doing it—for fear, I suppose, that I would fling his favors back in his face. But I was in the wrong; and now, that I am sure of it, I'm going to take the first opportunity I can find to tell him so." •

"And a capital thing, too ! " exclaimed the Captain cordially.   " I'm delighted to hear it ! "

By this time they had reached the head of Wall Street, where it debouches on Broadway ; and this spot, which is always full of movement, was to-day much more crowded than usual ; the bulk of the current setting down the narrow street, though there were eddies, momentarily stationary, here and there, and also an occasional opposition current, where persons with hurried steps and urgent faces forced their way through the crowd, or glided in and out with cunning evasions, like the arguments of some super-subtle attorneys.

As Cowran and his companion worked their way down the street, the press became momentarily greater and the noise of voices more noticeable, while ever and anon louder exclamations or calls rose above the general level of clamor. At the point where Wall Street joins Broad Street, a scene opened out which no one could contemplate without partaking in a greater or less degree of the prevailing excitement. The last-named thoroughfare deserves its name, being more like a long square than a street ; and it was filled to the brim with a crowd of men who were rushing in all directions at once, aimlessly to all appearance, but in reality upon most genuine and definite business.   Here the roar that had been loud in Wall Street took on a broader and fuller volume of sound, that filled the ear and made the brain vibrate. The throng was most dense and at the same time most active in front of the portico of a building with a white marble façade, that stood on the west side of the street near the Wall Street corner. A short flight of steps led up to this door, and upon, and down, and across, and round those steps, and in and out of the door, a human surf beat and rolled and spouted forth, and hurtled in, as if the greatest treasure and the greatest honor in the world were both hidden behind the portals. Men fought with obstinate determination to get in, and others leaped forth with white faces, and in frantic haste, as though Satan himself were at their heels. It was strange, in the midst of this bewildering turmoil, to look at the marble front of the building, with a blank, impassive countenance, lifting itself above the din and struggle with the quiet indifference of the dead.

"We can't get in that way," shouted Cowran in his companion's ear. "We must try the side door."

They turned, and struggled up the street again, and after a quarter of an hour's brisk conflict, they forced their way into the Exchange by a comparatively unfrequented route, in the passage of which, however, Cowran had his silk hat crushed as flat as a soup-plate, and one of the Captain's coat-tails was nearly severed from the garment to which it appertained. Both of the men were quite out of breath, and, though the temperature was considerably below the freezing-point, they were in a profuse perspiration.

"We got through that well !" gasped Cowran, endeavoring to straighten out his head-gear. "Now, then, up we go ; and when we get into the gallery don't be afraid to use your elbows !"

So saying, he led the way up to the staircase, passed a door, and, closely followed by the Captain, emerged into a balcony or gallery that partly surrounded a spacious and lofty hall. The gallery was filled with spectators; but Cowran shouldered them aside with scant ceremony, and at last succeeded in wedging himself and Hamilton into a position immediately in contact with the railing. From there they looked down upon the arena beneath.

Every thing that they had seen outside dwindled into insignificance in comparison with the spectacle that was here displayed. Every part of the great hall was dense with human bodies packed like nine-pins in a box, but each and all wriggling, twisting, fighting, raging, flinging their arms above their heads, diving, plunging, wrestling ; the air was tortured with yells, screams, shrieks, howls as of mortal agony, desperate cries, and appeals as of souls in torment screeching for their lives. The crowd was like one vast animal, struggling and crushing itself in myriad-fold fury, and quickening into a keener agony of life with each convulsion. At certain points in the hall this seeming blind and maddened frenzy was even denser and wilder than elsewhere, though that would appear impossible ; and in the very midst and red-hot center of the

demoniac ring—a miracle of calm in the acme of
tempest—would stand a single individual, quiet,
composed, languid, with a tablet and a pencil, jot-
ting down a figure or a word with lazy indifference,
or glancing out upon the serried ring of frantic
madmen with meditative eyes, as if recalling some
half-forgotten verse of poetry, or seeking for a syllable to polish off a rhyme of his own. These phil-
osophers apeared as remote from all participation
in the deafening dance of insanity that swept
around them as if they were denizens of the
planet Neptune, or, like the enchanters of old, had
drawn around them the magic circle, across which
the mob of hell could not pass, and, standing within
which, all their striving and uproar were invisible
and inaudible.

There were several of these whirlpools on the
floor of the great hall ; but gradually one of them
seemed to swallow up and absorb the rest ; and
upon this chief center all the rage and passion of
all the former centers were concentrated and heaped
up and welded together, until it seemed as if
human nature and strength could endure no more.
If the universe had been shattered to fragments,
and the inhabitants of this and of all other planets
had been emptied pell-mell into a pit, and told that
they were doomed to eternal torture unless they
obtained something unobtainable within the next
thirty seconds, they would have conducted themselves with more order and decorum. The whole
essence of chaos and anarchy seemed to pos-

sess each individual ; and yet, wonderful to relate, each individual had a very clear idea of what he was doing, and of what he had done and was likely to do ; he knew just what was going on, what it all meant, at what point it might be expected to change ; he was ready, between the throbs of the delirium, to turn aside and exchange a jest and a smile with an acquaintance, or to retire to a corner and have a little quiet conversation with a business associate, and perhaps give or receive an invitation to discuss a bird and a bottle after the Exchange closed.   Then, of a sudden, he would leap back into the ring, and be instantly transformed into a ferocious and chaotic maniac.

" What the deuce are they doing ? " shrieked the Captain into Cowran's tympanum.

" Oh, nothing," the other replied. " Somebody is running up Pacific Mail, and it has risen nearly thirty points in two hours.   It'll turn before long.   It isn't serious.   They're just having a little fun.   You should see 'em when they're in earnest."

" You're not concerned in it, I fancy ? " said the Captain.

" Me ?   Not much !   It's a long time since I've meddled with any thing of that kind.   Now-a-days, when I want to throw away money, I take a Jersey City ferry-boat and drop it into the middle of North River.   It's less trouble."

There was now a comparative lull for a few moments, during which the whirlpools broke up, and there was an extraordinary running to and fro

and erratic confusion, as if the moorings of all nature had broken loose and each fragment was hurrying to escape. Presently, with a roar that outdid
all previous efforts, the vortices began to form
again, and the bears began to tear down what the
bulls had just been hoisting up.

"Come," said Cowran, after a while, "we have
seen about all there is to be seen here to-day. They
will keep this up for another hour or two, and then
the whole thing will end exactly where it began. A
few of them will have won, and the rest will have
lost; and next week there will be another scrimmage of the same kind. Have you had enough?
Then come along."

They made their way out to the street, and
thence to Broadway, where they parted, Cowran
going to his office, and the Captain proceeding up
town. He stopped at the Astor House, however,
and there, in the course of an hour or so, he was
joined by a slender young man with sharp features,
who nodded to him and then went to the water-
cooler and swallowed a couple of glasses of water.

"Hot work!" he muttered, as he dropped into a
chair beside the Captain. "I'd rather pitch a dozen
championship games of an afternoon, or spend the
day in a foot-ball scrimmage!"

"Well, how did it work? Have you caught
him?"

"Caught him? No! He couldn't have been in
the thing at all. I can't understand it. Either
something has happened to him, or he got wind of

the game, and made up his mind to stay out of it."

" Then we're just as wise as we were before ? "

" Say a bit wiser ; for we know now that we know nothing ! "

CHAPTER XXI.

ARREST.

THE stock operation above alluded to took place on a Friday. On the following Sunday, General Weymouth, who had been unusually busy during the previous week, and had not once had an opportunity of indulging himself with his violoncello, dressed himself with especial care, put a bundle of documents in his pocket, and walked down Lexington Avenue to Kitty Clive's.

Kitty was in, and was writing a letter. She slipped it into an envelope as he entered.

"Whenever you come I feel that I have been wanting to see you," she said, coming forward and giving him her hand.

"Then I must not come too often," was his reply.

She laughed. "Oh, yes, come oftener. For it is when I have been trying to be good that I most enjoy having you here ; and so, the more you are here, the better I shall be !"

"That is rather shaky logic, I'm afraid, my dear young lady ; and yet, any logic must be good that affords me a pretext for seeing you. But, I should not have ventured to disturb you this morning, had I not depended upon my errand for my apology. I want to give myself—that is, you—a little pleasure."

"If my pleasure is yours, General, I wish I were the happiest woman alive!"

"There is no reason that I know of why you should not be. There is nothing in your own nature to make you otherwise; and though the world — your personal world—may not in all respects have been what it should have been to you hitherto, yet I am persuaded that this defect will sooner or later be amended. Perhaps quite soon," he added; "perhaps——" he looked at her closely, and interpreted some sign that she could not wholly disguise in her face—"perhaps the best that we hoped for is in sight already!"

She met his eyes a moment, was about to speak, checked herself with a sigh, and looked down.

"Do not think I want to pry into your secrets," he said quietly; "but I need not tell you how happy I should be to see you have what you wish— as I am sure you must and will have it before long."

"I feel that you are the truest of friends," she returned. "But at present I can only say this— that the means of the happiness you refer to have been put within my reach. And yet there are cir- cumstances that prevent my accepting it; perhaps I may always be prevented."

An expression of contentment lighted up the

general's face, which, as Kitty now noticed, was thinner and paler than usual.

"Possibly," he said, "my errand this morning may have the effect of removing some of the obstacles that lie in your way. It was with that expectation that I came here. But first I must tell you about something, quite unlooked for, that has lately occurred to me. You perhaps recollect my speaking to you the other day of a man whom I called Fowler ? "

Kitty moved her head in assent. She could foresee, of course, the gist of what the General was about to tell her ; but the ambiguous circumstances which had attended the last act of Fowler Morgan's life made her unwilling to let him suspect that she knew any thing about the matter.

"I had heard nothing about him for several years," the General went on ; "and so far as I thought of him at all, which was very little, I presumed that he was either dead, or had been overtaken in some manner by the just reward of his iniquity. It is only within the last few days that I learned any thing of his subsequent history and the only part of that which concerns my present purpose in coming here, is that he has just died, leaving behind him a considerable fortune.

"If I had been asked," the General continued, after a pause, "what was the thing, possible to be done, which that man would be least likely to do, I should have said that it was to make reparation in any respect for the injury that he had done me.

I need not tell you that the worst injury—the only injury that touched a vital part—could never be repaired or compensated ; he could never give me back the faith and peace of my early marriage. Nor could he give me back my ruined career, and all those schemes for doing good in the world for which I had hoped so much and striven so hard. The most that he could do was to return me the money which he had extorted from me. That money, were it ten times as much as it is, could have little value for me personally now ; I could not spend it on myself, and I am too old, and too long accustomed to solitude and inaction, to think of attempting any public activity again. But, on the other hand, he no doubt imagined that the loss of the money was what I chiefly cared for, and that in giving it back he acquitted himself of all his obligations. That he should wait to make the restitution until death had placed him where money has no existence, was a matter of course. It is surprising enough, as I said, that he should have made it even then.

" Nevertheless, that is what has happened. I received last week a letter from a firm of lawyers in Boston, informing me of the death of Fowler Morgan—such was the man's real name—and that his will bequeathed to me his entire property, with some trifling exceptions. The amount is large— vastly larger than I could ever use, or would wish to be burdened with. But for a single consideration, therefore, I should regret that Fowler Morgan's will was drawn in my favor."

He paused, and turned his face upon Kitty with a sort of deprecating expression, as if appealing to her in advance not to reject the proposition he was about to offer. It was not difficult for her to surmise what that proposition was to be, and she had no very clear idea how to meet it.

"I have here," said the General, feeling in his pocket, and bringing out some papers, which he laid across his knee while putting on his eyeglasses, "one or two documents which only require your approval and signature to become valid. As you see, a hundred and fifty thousand dollars have been deposited in the America Bank, subject to your order. This is the receipt; and if, at any time you feel inclined, you will write your name on that paper, and send it to the bank, you will afterwards be able to draw upon the sum as suits your convenience. You see, my dear Kitty, I feel a fatherly interest in you—being without daughters or relatives of my own—and as Christmas is not far off I want to take advantage of the season. I want you to feel that by indulging me in this little matter, which I have much at heart, you will be relieving me of a disagreeable responsibility—a regular white elephant—which, but for you, would rob me of my peace and comfort for the rest of my days. If I were as young and vigorous as you, I should think twice, I dare say,

before doing so wise, and, after all, sc selfish a thing
as I am doing now."

"You give me all this money, General Weymouth!" exclaimed Kitty, whose anticipations
had been limited to less than a tithe of this sum,
and whose perplexity at the actual denouement was
proportionately increased. "I can not take it. I
have no need of such a gift ; and if I had, my need
could not be relieved in such a way."

The General's hands dropped lifelessly on his
knees, and a look of heavy and bitter disappoint-
ment shadowed his face. "Don't say that!" he
murmured in a husky tone. "Don't say you won't
take any thing from me! I have had so many dis-
appointments, my dear ; and I am an old man,
now—more than old enough to be your father.
I don't see how I could bear to be disappointed in
this. Be a good, kind little daughter, now, and do
me this one favor! Surely you can not imagine
that I would ever take any advantage—that it
would be putting you under obligations—"

"No, no, nothing of that sort is in my mind,"
interrupted she passionately. She was deeply
moved, and did not seem to know how to express
herself. "I know what you are—there could be
no man more unselfish and single-hearted. But it
is because I do know it that I can tell you, without your misunderstanding me, that I can not take
your money. If—if I could have married you,
General Weymouth—that is the only thing that
would justify me in my own eyes in accepting it.

And since, if I ever do marry, it will be some one else—how could I go to him with the feeling that what I brought him was due to the love which another man had done me the honor to bear me? And you have misunderstood what I hinted of the obstacles that lay between him and me. It is not that there would not be money enough. I make money enough for both of us, if that were all; but he too is going to work; and even if there were no hope of either of us ever becoming comfortable in that way, I would not hesitate—it would be a delight to live poor with him, and be a mere household drudge, if he were the master of the house! But we have already all that we need, and we shall have more; and it is not that that made me silent when he asked me for my love the other day. Oh, not that!"

"I can not understand, then," said the General, with a slight gesture of the hand.

"I can not tell you," she rejoined, "for I have not yet told him; only I will say this, that the reason is a personal one—it relates to me, to what I am, to my life and character. I know," she continued, seeing an expression of indignant incredulity appear in the General's face. "I know that such words are capable of the worst interpretation. I do not deny or affirm any thing about that—you must judge by what you know of me—and that is very little! For, even if the good you think you see in me were all there, there would still be things that you have never seen—because you bring only what is best in me to the surface. If you were an enemy—if you had wronged me,' or injured any one I loved—then you might see what would make you shrink and stand aloof ! Do you think I would shrink from any crime if the man I loved—any one that was dear to me—had been unjustly treated ? Why, General Weymouth, in such a cause I would do murder !"

The old man sat quiet and motionless while she spoke thus ; and after she had ended there was a silence, disturbed only by her labored breath, as she tried to choke back the passion and the tears that were rising within her. But at last he said, in a voice that was all gentleness and sympathy : "My child, I understand you better now, and I thank you for the new depth to which you have admitted me. I will take it that you have committed some sin for the sake of the man you love, and that you now fear that the consequences of it may separate you. What the sin may be, I have no conception, nor is it needful that I should. I will only say that, if I may speak so far of a man I have never seen, I do not think that he will love you the less for what you have done. But whether or not, I counsel you most earnestly to tell him all, and at once ; and then, so far as may be possible, undo the evil you have committed. Few women have ever lived, Miss Kitty, who had such a heart as yours ; let an old fellow entreat you to subdue its fiercer part ; it can only sap the life of the diviner side. Do not worry yourself by assuming to administer God's justice. The best result that can ever come from doing so is to accept the warning it will bring you, never to assume that awful function again!"

He spoke with a solemnity and earnestness such as she had never heard from him before; and the profound and unselfish affection that enriched every word touched and softened her, so that she began to weep, not violently but quietly, leaning her head against the cushion of the sofa. A crisis seemed to have passed; and the old general was the good angel who had helped her safely through it.

He remained meditatively in his chair for a while, as if reviewing all that had passed, and asking himself whether there were any thing more to do. At length he rose, replaced the papers in his pocket, and took up his hat and gloves.

"As regards that other affair, my dear," he said, "I will not urge it upon you at present. You are the best judge of what is easy and graceful for you, and I certainly can claim no right to force upon you any special kind or condition of comfort, that I may fancy would be agreeable to me in your place. But after your marriage I shall, I hope, see you and your husband occasionally; and perhaps, between the three of us, we may contrive some expedient by which all three can be satisfied. With such a good and sensible fellow as I am sure he is that can not be impossible or even difficult. Meanwhile I will take myself off, wishing you all

the happiness in the world, provided it be of the
sort that you happen to approve of l "

She answered the smile with which he said this,
and gave him her hand ; but then said, " If you
will wait for me a moment, I will not say good-by
to you here. I have promised to sing in the
church at the corner to-day, and it is time I was
there. I will not keep you long."

She was as good as her word, and came out of
her room dressed for the street in a very short
time. Before they went out, she cast a glance
round the sitting-room, and seeing the letter she
had been writing lying on the desk, she took
it up and put it in her muff. They went downstairs together and turned up the street, not
noticing Captain Hamilton, who was approaching
from the opposite direction. He followed along
about fifty yards behind them. They stopped at
the door of the church, to say good-by ; and Kitty,
in taking her hand from her muff, was reminded
of her letter.

" Let me post it for you," said the General. " I
shall be sure to pass a letter-box in a few minutes."
She handed him the letter, which he put in the side-
pocket of his overcoat, and they parted. She
entered the church ; the General turned towards
Fifth Avenue.

The noiseless footsteps of fate came close behind him. At the junction of Twenty-second Street
with Fifth Avenue was a letter-box attached to a
lamp-post : and into this box the General dropped

the letter. He then turned up the Avenue, and proceeded northward. Before he had gone a dozen yards two men overtook him, one of whom placed a hand on his shoulder, and, as the General looked round in surprise, said, "I have to inform you, sir, that you are in custody. You must go with us to Inspector Byrnes' office."

CHAPTER XXII.

DISTRICT E.

IN order to an understanding of this event, we must turn backwards a day or two, and find out what Inspector Byrnes had been doing.

The chief of the detectives had been not a little piqued by the failure of himself and his subordinates to solve the mystery of the blackmailing letter-writer ; and he determined to make a final effort to get at the heart of the problem. All the ordinary methods in vogue in such cases, and several that were not ordinary, had been tried without effect ; and the artificial panic on the Exchange, out of which so much had been hoped, had given not the slightest clew to the offender ; who had, apparently, —for what reason it was impossible to conjecture —not operated on that occasion at all, although, had he done so, he might have made a very large sum of money. As it was, several outsiders had been enriched, many innocent people had suffered loss, and nothing whatever had come of it.

" This will never do ! " said the Inspector to himself, as he paced up and down his room, at an hour when most of the inhabitants of the city had closed up their business for the day and gone home to dinner and relaxation. " This will never do ! " he repeated. " There must be some way of getting hold of that fellow, and I must find out what it is. Come ! common sense can find its way through any thing ! Where is the weak spot in that fellow's armor ? He has written over twenty letters ; isn't there a single clew in any one of them ? or in all of them put together ? "

He took half a dozen more turns up and down, thinking intently. The room was perfectly quiet, and the Inspector's footfall on the soft carpet gave out no sound. The curtains were drawn ; the lights burned brightly ; the glazed cases on the walls, full of the relics of former crimes, reflected in dis. torted fragments the movements of the detective as he paced to and fro—five paces this way, a turn, and five paces back again. At length he stopped, went behind the table, and sat down in his chair.

" Let us see ! " he muttered. " We know it is not Cowran ; we know it is not Cunliffe ; and no one else has been suggested. We have tried decoy advertisements, and they have only served to induce the fellow to continue his letters ; we have tried manipulating the stocks in which he was interested ; and if he has profited by the information given him, he has left no trace by which we could follow him. We have offered to give him checks or money, and he has refused the offer. We have attempted to lure him into communicating with us in some other way than by advertisements, and he has declined the proposition. What else is there to be done? One might, by accident, happen to see him in the act of posting one of his letters ; only, one would have to have a quick eye to read the address while the letter was being popped into the box : and if one were near enough to do it, the fellow would probably either not post it at all, or else do it in such a way that the address would be invisible. Besides, there are two or three thousand letter-boxes in the city,—no, that is impracticable. And, even if a man were seen to post a letter addressed to Maxwell Golding, that would not justify his arrest. Mr. Golding has more correspondents than one, or than one hundred. To be sure, if the address were in the handwriting of the blackmail letters, that would be another matter ! And if—ah ! if ! "

He leaned back in his chair, folded his arms, and closed his eyes. A person entering the room might have imagined the Inspector to be asleep. But he was very far from that.

His thoughts ran as follows :—" If the fellow is, as he appears to be, a resident of the city, and ac-customed to observe a certain routine in his life, then it is probable that he would not go out of a cer-tain definite region ; say, a region bounded by Sixth Avenue on the west, Third Avenue on the east, north by Forty-second Street, and south by Wall Street. That is giving him a large range ; there are thousands of business and club men who are hardly ever met with off Fifth Avenue or Broad-way. Thus, all the space between, say, Fourteenth

Street and City Hall may be stricken out, for he
will pass over that in the cars. During business
hours he would be below City Hall, and at other
times above Fourteenth Street. But he would not
be likely to write his blackmailing letters at his
club, or at his place of business. No ; he would
do that at home. Well, his house may be anywhere. But I take it that he is an unmarried man,
and therefore would live in lodgings or in a board-
ing house in a good quarter of the town ; somewhere above Thirtieth and below Forty-second ;
not further west than Sixth or Seventh avenue, and
—well—probably not east at all. Somewhere in
that region the letters are written—and somewhere
in that region they are posted, for he would not
carry them about with him any longer than was
necessary. In fact, it is quite likely that he may
have posted every one of the letters in the same
box ! But the stamp shows only the district, not
the box. Still, it would be something to know
that they were all posted in the same district ; and
that I can find out right here ! Why didn't I
think of it before ? "

At this point the Inspector opened his eyes,
which had a new sparkle of expectancy in them, and
pulled out a small private drawer in the recesses
of the desk, which contained a score or more of
letters in their envelopes. They were the
entire correspondence of the anonymous blackmailer, up to date. They were all addressed to Maxwell Golding, in a scrawling, irreg-

ular hand, evidently disguised, but as evidently by
the same writer in every case. Each envelope
bore the stamp of the district office at which it was
received. The Inspector examined these stamps
one after another. The first was " E," so was the
second. So likewise was the third. The fourth
was " E " again, and the fifth and the sixth.
" Why, upon my word," explained the Inspector,
after a moment, " they are nearly all ' E ' ! " So
far, at any rate, I don't seem to be much astray.
Now let us see whereabouts ' E ' is ! "

From another drawer in the table he got out a
large map of New York city, with the districts
marked upon it. A brief inspection revealed the
fact that district ' E ' comprises that portion of the
city's area which is bounded on the north by
Forty-third Street, on the south by Twenty-first
street, east by Fifth Avenue, and west by the North
River.

" That is a tolerably large territory," said the Inspector to himself, " but at any rate it comprises the
place where I supposed my man to be living. Now,
how am I to find out which particular letter-box
he uses? It can not be done. However, he evidently uses some one of the boxes in that district.
How many are there ? "

A postal directory was lying on the table : and
a consultation of it showed that district ' E ' contained just 118 letter boxes.

" One hundred and eighteen is a good many,"
the Inspector mused, " but it is much more easily

managed than two or three thousand. If I could set a watch on every one of those boxes, something might come of it. But there are not so many detectives in the office. No; but perhaps the post-office authorities could be induced to send me fifty or sixty men to help me out. Well, but they could be spared for only one day at most; and how do I know that the blackmailer would post a letter on that day? Pshaw! that is easy enough! Insert an urgent 'personal' in the paper that would require an immediate reply from him; set the watch on that day, and catch him! Yes; but suppose I have a man at every box, near enough to see the address of the letter as it goes in, is it not as good as certain that the fellow will notice it and take the alarm? On the other hand, if they are stationed at a distance, how are they to know what the address is? That is an obstacle! Let us see if there is no way around it."

He leaned his head on his hand and pondered earnestly for over a minute.

"I have it!" he suddenly exclaimed; "the thing is as simple as possible! let each of the men have a key, and take up his position half-a-dozen yards away from the box to which he is assigned. As soon as any one posts a letter, and starts to go away, the watcher comes forward and opens the box. If the letter just dropped in is to Golding, arrest the man! Is there any thing wrong with that?"

Again he meditated intently: and an expression of

chagrin overspread his features. " There is a difficulty," he muttered, " and though it seems a trifling
one, it is enough to upset the whole scheme. If
the first, or second, or third letter posted in the
box should be to Golding, it would be all right.
But it is more likely to be the fiftieth or sixtieth.
In that case, when the box is opened, the watcher
will have to look through the whole pile of letters to
discover whether the one he wants is among them :
and by the time he has done that, the blackmailer
will be half-a-dozen blocks away. That must be
remedied—but how ? If only the letters already
posted could in some way be separated from the
one posted last. To be sure, each letter might be
taken out as it was posted, and kept out. But that
would hardly do ; it would involve letting all the
carriers into the scheme. No—we must think of
something else. How to distinguish at a glance
the last letter posted from the others ? There must
be a method, if I could but hit upon it. The other
letters must be in a heap by themselves, and the last
one—Ah! I see it now! and that concludes the whole
matter. Here is the solution," and the Inspector
took up an ordinary india-rubber band, such as
everyone uses in making up packets of papers. " Let
one of them be slipped round the letters as fast as
they are examined. Thus, every time the box is
opened, there will always be a bundle of letters and a
loose letter. The loose letter will be the one last put
in, and the watchers can see at a glance whether it is
addressed to Maxwell Golding. Yes, that settles

it. The thing can be done, and it shall be done without the loss of a day. I will make my application to the post-office at once, and on Sunday, which is somewhat of an off-day for the men, we will put the scheme to the test. So now to work!"

Summoning an assistant, Inspector Byrnes's first act was to cause a diagram or map of District E to be prepared, with every letter-box marked in red on its proper site. It then appeared that several of the boxes were so situated that one watcher could attend to two of them, and thus less than a hundred men in all would be required.

A "personal" was then despatched to the paper, upbraiding the blackmailer with having given away to others the secret information regarding the variations in stocks which had been intended for him alone. As a matter of fact, there was no reason to suppose that he had done any thing of the kind ; but, whether he had or not, he would be certain to lose no time in repudiating the charge, and thus the success of the scheme on the particular day selected would be ensured.

The next morning application was made to the post-office authorities for permission to employ in the work as many of their men as could be spared, the Detective Bureau paying all expenses. With some difficulty, this permission was obtained for a detail of fifty men. As many more of the detective staff were selected ; and at six o'clock on the Sunday morning the whole squad of one hundred were admitted to the Inspector's room. He addressed them, carefully explaining to them every circumstance of the plan, and assigning to each the letter-box which he was to watch. It was arranged that when the fatal letter was posted, the man who discovered should make a signal by raising his hat, upon which the detective in attendance should proceed to arrest the person who had posted it.

Every thing having now been prepared, so far as human ingenuity could prepare it, the men were despatched to their posts, and the watch began.

The Inspector sat in his office and waited. Outwardly, he appeared in his calmest and sunniest humor; but we may be permitted to surmise that, had his mind been visible through his face, a certain amount of suspense and anxiety would have been observable. In truth, there was a great deal at stake, not least among which was the Inspector's confidence in his own abilities. If he were to fail now, he must acknowledge himself beaten ; and to be beaten was something to which the Inspector had never had an opportunity to become accustomed. Was his Waterloo to come to-day ? He lit a cigar and breathed a modest hope that, if it turned out a Waterloo indeed, he would be found to have acted the part of a Wellington rather than of a Napoleon.

The Inspector smoked several cigars.

As he was in the act of lighting a fresh one, there was a loud knock at the door, and two officers entered, leading between them an elderly, dignified man, with dark eyes and an iron-gray mustache.

CHAPTER XXIII.

KITTY CLIVE.

THE Inspector took his cigar from his mouth, straightened himself in his chair, and bent a quiet and impassive look upon his visitor. There was no sign of triumph in his gaze, not even any betrayal of unusual interest. And yet here was the man whom he had been pursuing with all the means and intelligence at his command for weeks, and whom he had captured just at the moment when pursuit seemed hopeless. And so this noble-appearing gentleman was the author of those out-rageous letters, — a blackmailer, — an anonymous threatener. Never did appearances so belie character.

There was something familiar in the prisoner's appearance, which puzzled the Inspector for a moment, and sent him hunting among the archives of his memory. Where had he seen the man before? Ah! he remembered now. It was this man who had stopped him on Fifth Avenue and asked him for a light for his cigar, on the evening when the Inspector was on his way to hear from Mr. Owens the first news of the crime.

After putting a few routine questions to the

detectives, who testified that they had arrested the
prisoner in the act of posting a letter to Mr. Golding, which letter they produced, the Inspector
made them a sign to retire; and, having dispatched
a messenger to request the attendance of Mr. Golding and Mr. Owens, he turned to his prisoner, and
asked him his name.

" My name is Weymouth," he replied. " I am a
retired army officer.   I do not yet know why I have
been brought here."

" There is no need of my beating about the bush
with you, General Weymouth," replied the Inspector, gravely.   " If the evidence against you were not
complete, it might be necessary to induce you to
commit yourself.   You posted this letter to Mr.
Golding this morning ? "

" I did ; but I was not aware that it was addressed to "——he got thus far and then stopped.
" I am not aware that it is illegal to write to Mr.
Golding," he said after a moment ; "nor do you
know the contents of that envelope."

" The contents of this particular envelope are
immaterial.   But that letter is the last of a series
which you have addressed to Mr. Golding during
the past four or five weeks."   As he spoke he took
the letters in question from a drawer and spread
them on the table.   The prisoner glanced at them
and then at the Inspector.   He seemed slightly perplexed, but betrayed no sign of guilty consternation.

" As you see," continued the detective, " this

letter, which you admit having posted, is in the same handwriting as the others."

" So it appears," returned the other, composedly. "So far as I am concerned, however, I never until this moment saw or knew any thing about any of those letters except the last."

" You did not write them yourself ? "

" I did not ; nor do I know a word that is in any of them."

" Not even in the last ? "

" Not even in that."

" As regards the last, we shall learn its contents when Mr. Golding arrives here and opens it. The others, as you know, General Weymouth, are a series of blackmailing communications of the worst character, demanding money from Mr. Golding under threats of murder. It is not in my power, nor is it my purpose, to save you from any part of the penalty appointed for the crime which you have committed. But I need not say that I have no personal animosity in this case ; and I see that you are a gentleman by position and education, whatever you may be otherwise. And I will tell you that if you make a clean breast of the affair you will spare yourself some unpleasant formalities. If you refuse (as of course you have a perfect right to do), you must be searched and in all respects treated as an ordinary malefactor."

To the latter part of this speech the prisoner did not seem to have paid any attention. At the word " blackmailing " he had given a start, and a great

and painful change had come over his countenance,
as if he had heard of the death or destruction of all
that was dearest to him. From that moment he
remained staring at the letters on the table with a
sort of bewildered consternation. After the Inspector ceased speaking there was a silence.

"What is your decision?" the latter inquired at
length.

The other drew a long breath, and steadied himself by a manifest effort. He raised his head and
looked the detective in the face. He opened his
lips to speak, but it was only after several attempts
that his voice became audible.

"I—submit—to the—logic of circumstances,"
he said, with a labored utterance. "I have—no
defense to make." He swayed on his feet as he
spoke, and grasped at a chair to sustain himself.

"Sit down," the Inspector said. "You have
decided wisely, and you will at least lose nothing
by it. I will write out the memoranda."

The General sank into a chair, breathing pain-
fully, and the Inspector took pen and paper and
began to write. While he was in the midst of this
employment there was a knock at the door and
Mr. Golding was admitted, followed by Courtlandt
Owens.

The great financier of his time was at this period
but little past the prime of life, and seemed
likely to more than outlast the allotted span of
human existence. His face was colorless, but the
flesh was firm and healthy ; there were no gray

threads in his thick black hair ; and his blue eyes, deep-set, were as bright and clear as the eyes of youth. His figure, rather under the middle height, but noticeably broad in the shoulders, was compact and upright ; his hands, with their long, square-topped fingers, were characteristic of the strength of his nature, his patience, his pertinacity, and his wonderful organizing power. He was simply dressed in a gray frock coat, buttoned across his chest, and a dark overcoat ; and the hat which he removed on entering was a little the worse for wear.

He bowed to the Inspector, and then nodded familiarly to General Weymouth. "I have come," he said, in a deep, low voice, "in answer to your message stating that this blackmailer had been arrested. Is he in the building ?"

"He is here, Mr. Golding," replied the detective, with a movement of the head towards the silent figure in the chair.

"I see no one," said Golding, with a glance around the room,—"except my friend General Weymouth," he added, with a smile.

The Inspector was silent. After a moment, Golding's expression changed. His face became as hard and inscrutable as a mask of stone.

"Do I understand that General Weymouth is the author of those letters ?" he demanded sharply.

"He was arrested in the act of mailing the last one, and he does not deny his guilt," was the answer.

Golding turned to the General. "How is this, Weymouth?" he said.

The old man fixed his dark eyes upon the financier. "I have nothing to say," he remarked, after a short pause. "The Inspector has spoken for me."

Golding pressed his lips together, and a gloomy expression darkened over his features. "I was not expecting this," he said at length. "General Weymouth called on me a month or two ago—I knew him well formerly—and asked me to find him some salaried position. I told him I could not do it; but I offered him a considerable sum of money from my private purse to serve as his support. Is that not so, Weymouth?"

"You offered me a hundred thousand dollars," the latter replied, "and I refused it."

"That being the case," Golding continued, "I don't understand why you should afterwards try to extort money from me by illegal means. Why was it?"

"I have nothing to say," repeated the other.

Here Owens approached the Inspector and asked in a low voice, "Has any incriminating evidence been found upon him?"

"The examination has not yet been made; I wished Mr. Golding to see him first." He turned to the General and said, "You are required by law to show any papers or other articles in your possession."

This announcement evidently disconcerted the

prisoner. "There is nothing in my possession," he said, in an agitated tone, "that has any bearing on this case. I do not deny that I have committed the crime charged. I entreat that my papers—that I be not subjected to an examination. Golding, I beg you will not ask it. " Does not my admission satisfy you ? "

" I can not interfere with the course of the law," Golding replied coldly. " If your papers are not incriminating, you can have no reason for not showing them."

" I entreat you not to ask it," the old man repeated.

" Mr. Golding has no voice in the matter," the Inspector interposed. " I request you to show me your papers. Do not force me to demand them."

The General put his hand in the inside pocket of his coat and brought out some documents, which he laid on the table. " Take them, if it is your duty," he said. " I have done what I could." He then folded his arms, bent his head upon his breast, and seemed to sink into a state of semi-lethargy.

The Inspector opened the documents and examined them. Presently he looked up and signed to Golding and Owens to approach.

" These appear to be vouchers and receipts for the sum of one hundred and fifty thousand dollars, held on deposit in The America Bank, subject to the order of one Kitty Clive," he said. " The deposit was made yesterday, by General Weymouth, and the signature of Kitty Clive is all that is needed to complete the transaction. Is the person of that name known to either of you?"

Golding shook his head. But Owens said, " I think there is a singer of that name ; I am under the impression that I have heard her in concert."

"The most obvious interpretation of the matter is," observed the detective, "that she is well known to General Weymouth, and that he has deeded this money to her, either as a *bonâ fide* gift or as a measure of security for himself. We do not know where the money came from ; but it is at least possible that it is the outcome of the stock operations which you have enabled the writer of those letters to make."

"I hardly think they can have been so extensive," Golding said.

"What we must do," continued the other, "is to find this Kitty Clive at once and question her. She may be able to throw an important light on the matter. For I must confess," he added in a lower tone, "that in spite of appearances, I think there is a good deal behind this affair. The prisoner's behavior and circumstances are hardly consistent with the facts as indicated by the evidence. I will send for this woman immediately."

He touched a bell ; but at the same moment the door opened, and Captain Hamilton entered, accompanied by a lady with a veil over her face. Of her own accord she removed this veil, revealing a plain but striking countenance, with gray eyes full of passion and resolution. As for the Captain, he wore a curiously dejected look, as of a man who has sacrificed something dear to him on the altar of abstract duty.

"Inspector," he said at once, before anyone else could speak. "I have important evidence to give in the matter which is now before you. Upwards of a week ago, I was in the house occupied by this lady, Miss Kitty Clive, on Lexington Avenue, where I saw on a blotting-pad on the table the name of Maxwell Golding reversed, as if printed off from the wet writing; and as near as I could judge, it was in the handwriting used in the blackmailing letters. I knew that Miss Clive was on terms of friendship with Frank Cunliffe, who was at that time suspected of being the author of the letters; I conjectured that he had written one of those letters in Miss Clive's house—as I presumed, without her knowledge or connivance. Subsequently it appeared that Mr. Cunliffe was probably not the author of the letters; but the testimony of the blotting book remained and gave me much trouble: for I could not think that Miss Clive was the guilty person. But I resolved to settle my doubts as to that, and with that view I went to Miss Clive's house this morning. As I approached it, she came out of the door, accompanied by the prisoner, General Weymouth. They did not see me, but walked on to the church at the corner. Miss Clive went into the church, but first she took out of her muff a sealed letter, which she gave to the General, apparently requesting him to post it for her. He took the letter and walked across town to.Fifth Avenue, then up to the corner of Twenty-second Street, where he seemed to recollect the letter, took it from his pocket, and slipped it into the letter-box on the lamp-post there. I had him in view all this time, and did not see him once look at the address on the letter. Immediately after he had posted it the box was opened by the person appointed for that duty, who took out the letter, and after reading the address, raised his hat, upon which two detectives arrested the prisoner. But in consequence of what I had seen, I returned to the church on Lexington Avenue, where Miss Clive was singing in the choir, obtained an interview with her, and informed her that she was under arrest. When learning the facts that I have stated, she at once agreed to accompany me here. I now have the honor to hand her over to you as my prisoner, on the charge of writing the blackmailing letters which Mr. Golding has received."

This statement, which was made in a rapid and mechanical tone, but with perfect distinctness, produced a sensation. The new prisoner alone appeared unmoved. She had stood looking alternately at the Inspector and at Mr. Golding, but had avoided turning her eyes upon the General.

" Do you admit the truth of Mr. Hamilton's statement ?" asked the Inspector.

" I do," she replied.

" Do you claim the authorship of the letters ? "

"I wrote them all," was her answer. "You will find evidence enough of it in my house ; meanwhile, here is the key of the cipher which was used in the correspondence." She took a slip of paper from her pocket-book, which she handed to the Inspector, who looked at it, and passed it to Mr. Golding.

"What induced you to write the letters ?" the detective demanded.

"My reasons are given in the letter posted this morning," was the reply.

"By the way, Mr. Golding," said the Inspector, "that letter has not been opened yet. Will you look at it ?" and he handed it to him.

Golding tore open the envelope, and read as follows :—

"Sir—This is the last letter you will receive from me. The money which I have obtained through your means was intended, not for myself, but for a dear friend of mine, whom you have ruined. I thought you ought to be punished and to make restitution ; if you had refused me information, I would have shot you. When I had collected the twenty thousand dollars which my friend lost, I meant to give them to him as the proceeds of my legitimate speculation, never letting him know the truth. But circumstances have convinced me that he would not wish to accept a gift of money from anyone, not even from me ; and I have also been made to feel that I was not justified in doing as I have done.

I believe that you were less culpable than I supposed, and that you do what is right ·according to the code by which you live. Therefore I have put the money made through your information in a bank, in your name, as you will see by the inclosed certificate. You will make what use of it you please ; I hope it may at least add to the unhappiness of no one." This was all, except a certificate showing a balance to Mr. Golding's credit of twenty one thousand five hundred dollars.

"What induced you to change your mind and return this money ?" demanded Golding, abruptly, facing round upon Kitty.

"It was chiefly the influence of that gentleman, Mr. Golding," she answered, indicating the General, who was leaning back in his chair, with a strange look in his face. "He is one of the best men that ever lived ; and it was the knowledge of his goodness that made me see my action toward you in a different light. He would have made me the heiress of the fortune that he himself received unexpectedly but a short time since ; and when I could not take it, and he saw that I was troubled because of something I had done, he gave me the counsel that determined me to give up my purpose. And I wish him to know that though, as fate would have it, I am a detected and disgraced criminal, —and though he himself, perhaps, would shrink from me now—yet I feel that I owe whatever is worth living for in my life to him ; and I would willingly undergo all the infamy and suffering that

may be in store for me for the sake of knowing
that he believes there is some good in me, and is
my friend."

The General had listened to these words with an
air of strained attention that was painful to see ;
and when, at the last sentence, she turned and
rested her eyes on him for the first time since her
entrance, he suddenly rose to his feet and held out
his arms, and a cry broke from him, inarticulate,
but so searching, tender, and compassionate that it
caused the tears to spring to the eyes of more than
one who heard it. The cry stopped abruptly, and
the General fell back into his chair, as if smitten
with death. Inspector Byrnes was beside him in
an instant, but not before Kitty Clive had
reached him. Her arm was round him, and his
head rested on her shoulder. " My friend—my
friend ! " she murmured ; " I have brought this
upon you ! "

The Inspector felt his pulse and looked in his
face. " It is paralysis," he said at last, "not death.
He will be better presently ; Hamilton, go call the
surgeon ; allow me, Miss Clive." He lifted the
stricken man in his strong arms, and laid him
gently on the sofa at the other side of the room.

Kitty watched him with yearning eyes ; then she
clasped her hands over her face and broke into
sobs. " Oh, I cannot nurse him—I shall not see
him again ! " she cried, in a wild tone ; " I brought
it on him—my friend—my friend ! "

Meanwhile, Mr. Golding and Owens had been

conversing apart, and the former now came forward.

" I have a word to say to you, Miss Clive," he
began, going up to her and putting his hand on
her shoulder ; she uncovered her face as she felt
his strong eyes resting upon her. " You have
been a naughty girl," he went on, " and I don't
mind saying that you have caused me some
uneasiness. But I don't believe you are a
hardened offender ; and as no one outside of this
room knows of your escapade I don't see that
any thing would be gained by sending you to prison.
The evidence is rather confusing, but as near as I
can make it out some young fellow in whom you
feel an interest has been dabbling in stocks, and
lost his money ; you undertook to set him right
and punish me at the same time ;—and now you
are afraid you can't marry him, because you have
been caught writing me wicked letters. Is that
about right ? well, I haven't the pleasure of this
young gentleman's acquaintance ; but all I have
to say is, if he doesn't want you, you may take it
that you are well rid of him ! a man who doesn't
know a woman when he sees one is a fool. But
if, on the contrary, he is not a fool, and does
want you, send him to me, and I will find something
better for him to do for a living than being
sheared on 'Change. As for this twenty thousand
dollars, it certainly doesn't belong to me ; and
since you have brought it into existence, I don't
see but you must be responsible for it. I hope

you will for once prove it an exception to the prov-
erb that ill-gotten gains bring ill results. Well,
that's all for the present; only, with the permission of Inspector Byrnes here, I think you had
better attend General Weymouth to his home, and
see that he is well taken care for there. He is a
good man, as you say; and I hope that for his
sake you will not believe all the evil of your fellow-
creatures that you may read in the newspapers or
hear from idle gossips. Even a financier may not
be in all respects a heartless scoundrel."

Half an hour later, the Inspector, Golding and
Owens were alone together in the office.

"This has been a very difficult and intricate
business, Inspector," Mr. Golding was saying, "and
I am much indebted to you for the masterly manner in which you have got to the bottom of it. It
only remains to ask you the amount of the expenses that you have incurred."

"The expenses amount to nothing."

"Nothing? no, no," returned Golding. "That's
no way to do business, and you'll never be a rich
man if you adopt it."

Inspector Byrnes smiled, and shook his head.
"I am just as much obliged to you," he said. "I
have simply done my duty as an officer, and the success of my stratagems is my reward."

"Well, there seems to be a difference between
Mulberry Street and Wall Street," remarked the
other, with a short laugh. "Money isn't quite so

much of a drug in the market there as here. Allow me to shake hands with you at any rate."

The two men grasped hands cordially, and Golding said, looking the detective straight in the face, " Inspector, if I ever can be of service to you, command me ! " Owens also bade him a hearty farewell, and the chief detective was left alone to meditate over all that had happened.

* * * * * *

So the Gordian knots of life untwist themselves, or are cut asunder by the sword of fate.

General Weymouth died six months after the last described events, tended constantly by a woman who had learned the meaning of gratitude, humility, and charity. What became of his fortune I have never been told, but I can conjecture.

John Talbot married Miss Betty Claverhouse the following autumn ; they received, as a marriage gift from a friend of theirs, twenty-one thousand five hundred dollars. Betty is somewhat more careful of her tongue than she used to be, but has not yet learned how to skate.

Captain Hamilton has left New York, and is believed to be in Africa. He can never hear the song of " Caller Herrin' " without inexplicable emotion.

Cunliffe has a good position on a railway. He is still unmarried. But he has never cared for but one woman, and never will.

THE END.

Pears'

Soap.

You Dirty Boy!

WHAT AILS YOU?

Do you feel dull, languid, low-spirited, lifeless, and indescribably miserable, both physically and mentally; experience a sense of fullness or bloating after eating, or of "goneness," or emptiness of stomach in the morning, tongue coated, bitter or bad taste in mouth, irregular appetite, dizziness, frequent headaches, blurred eyesight, "floating specks" before the eyes, nervous prostration or exhaustion, irritability of temper, hot flushes, alternating with chilly sensations, sharp, biting, transient pains here and there, cold feet, drowsiness after meals, wakefulness, or disturbed and unrefreshing sleep, constant, indescribable feeling of dread, or of impending calamity?

If you have all, or any considerable number of these symptoms, you are suffering from that most common of American maladies — Bilious Dyspepsia, or Torpid Liver, associated with Dyspepsia, or Indigestion. The more complicated your disease has become, the greater the number and diversity of symptoms. No matter what stage it has reached, **Dr. Pierce's Golden Medical Discovery** will subdue it, if taken according to directions for a reasonable length of time. If not cured, complications multiply, and Consumption of the Lungs, Skin Diseases, Heart Disease, Rheumatism, Kidney Disease, or other grave maladies are quite liable to set in, and, sooner or later, induce a fatal termination.

Dr. Pierce's Golden Medical Discovery

CURES ALL HUMORS,

from a common Blotch, or Eruption, to the worst Scrofula. Salt-rheum, "Fever-sores," Scaly or Rough Skin, in short, all diseases caused by bad blood, are conquered by this powerful, purifying, and invigorating medicine. Great Eating Ulcers rapidly heal under its benign influence. Especially has it manifested its potency in curing Tetter, Eczema, Erysipelas, Boils, Carbuncles, Sore Eyes, Scrofulous Sores and Swellings, Hip-joint Disease, "White Swellings," Goitre, or Thick Neck, and Enlarged Glands.

CONSUMPTION,

which is **Scrofula of the Lungs**, is arrested and cured by this remedy, if taken in the earlier stages of the disease.

For Weak Lungs, Spitting of Blood, Shortness of Breath, Chronic Nasal Catarrh, Bronchitis, Asthma, Severe Coughs, and kindred affections, it is an efficient remedy.

Sold by Druggists, at $1.00, or Six Bottles for $5.00.

World's Dispensary Medical Association,

No. 663 Main Street, BUFFALO, N. Y.

CASSELL & COMPANY, Limited,

104 & 106 FOURTH AVENUE, NEW YORK.